# STEVE HARTLEY

DANNY BAKER'S SILLY OLYMPICS

The Wibbly Wobbly Jelly Belly Flop

100% UNOFFICIAL!

## ILLUSTRATED BY KATE PANKHURST

MACMILLAN CHILDREN'S BOOKS

'The Toxic Toes' and 'The Baffled Brain Boffins' first published 2010 in *Danny Baker Record Breaker: The World's Biggest Bogey* by Macmillan Children's Books
'The Pain in Spain' and 'The Super-Secret Ingredient' first published 2010 in *Danny Baker Record Breaker: The World's Awesomest Air-Barf* by Macmillan Children's Books

This bind-up edition, plus new story 'The Wibbly Wobbly Jelly Belly Flop', published 2012 by Macmillan Children's Books
a division of Macmillan Publishers Limited
20 New Wharf Road, London N1 9RR
Basingstoke and Oxford
Associated companies throughout the world
www.panmacmillan.com

ISBN 978-1-4472-0812-9

Text copyright © Steve Hartley 2010, 2012
Illustrations copyright © Kate Pankhurst 2010, 2012

The right of Steve Hartley and Kate Pankhurst to be identified as the author and illustrator of this work has been asserted by them in accordance with the Copyright, Designs and Patents Act 1988.

1 3 5 7 9 8 6 4 2

A CIP catalogue record for this book is available from the British Library.

Printed and bound by CPI Group (UK) Ltd, Croydon CR0 4YY

REU

Please return/renew this item
by the last date shown.
Books may also be renewed by
phone or the Internet.

**Tel: 01253 478070**
**www.blackpool.gov.uk**

You can find out more about Steve

3 4114 00598 4454

*Other books by Steve Hartley*

DANNY BAKER RECORD BREAKER
The World's Loudest Armpit Fart

DANNY BAKER RECORD BREAKER
The World's Stickiest Earwax

DANNY BAKER RECORD BREAKER
The World's Itchiest Pants

DANNY BAKER RECORD BREAKER
The World's Windiest Baby

*For Rosie*

A giga-squig-squillion people have helped bring Danny Baker's mega-silly world to life in so many different ways. However, the following lovely ladies deserve special thanks:
My agent Sarah Manson,
My illustrator Kate Pankhurst,
My editors Emma Young and Samantha Swinnerton,
My daughters Rosie and Connie, and
My wife Louise, for her ace ideas, mega suggestions and for loving Danny as much as I do.

# Contents

# The Toxic Toes

# Bogey

To the Manager
The Great Big Book of World Records
London

Dear Sir

I have been collecting bogeys from my nose
for the last two years. I have stuck them all
together to make one enormous bogey. It
measures 5.3 cm in diameter and weighs 3.6 g.
Here is a photograph of me holding the bogey.
Is this a record?

Yours faithfully
Danny Baker
(Aged nine and a bit)

me and my bogey ↑

lick
my bogeys!

The Great Big Book
of World Records
London

ARE YOU A RECORD
BREAKER ?

Dear Danny Baker

Thank you for your letter about your big bogey. I am sorry to tell you that it is not a record.

Ronald Ramsbottom of Rawtenstall, Lancashire, is the Individual Bogey world-record holder. He was the All-England Nose-picking Champion for thirteen straight years, from 1982 to 1994. Unfortunately, in 1995 he chopped off his right index finger trying to unblock a jammed electric pencil sharpener. Ronald entered the championship that year using his left index finger, but came ninth. He retired, and now picks his nose only for fun. His collected bogeys measured 47 cm in diameter, and weighed 2.51 kg.

4

As a matter of interest, the biggest Team
Bogey ever created was one that measured
5.1 m in diameter and weighed 3,198.7 kg. It
took six years of continuous nose-picking by
467 boys from a school in Chichibu in Japan.
On the day they decided to stop picking their
noses, they invited their headmaster to add
the final bogey. Tragically, just as he put
his finger up his nose, a freak gust of wind
started the ball rolling. The headmaster and
fifteen of the boys were squashed to death.
Thirty-one other pupils had to go to hospital.
All of which goes to show that great care must
be taken when attempting to break *any* world
record.

Best wishes
Eric Bibby
Keeper of the Records

'Bad luck, Danny,' said his best
friend Matthew Mason. He
handed the letter back to
Danny and continued tying
up the laces on his football boots.

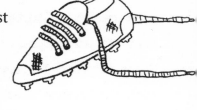

'Imagine being killed by a giant bogey. Gross.'

'Yeah,' agreed Danny. He pulled his green
goalkeeper's shirt over his head and tucked it into
his black shorts. He sighed and gazed dreamily
into space. 'I was going to
have my bogey
mounted on
a wooden
stand and
present it to
Penleydale
Museum.
They'd have
put it in
a small
glass case
with a sign

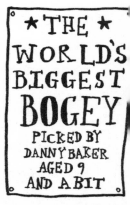

★ THE ★
WORLD'S
BIGGEST
BOGEY
PICKED BY
DANNY BAKER
AGED 9
AND A BIT

PLEASE
DO NOT
TOUCH

saying THE WORLD'S BIGGEST BOGEY, PICKED BY DANNY BAKER, AGED NINE AND A BIT.' Danny sighed again. 'I'd have to pick my nose for years to make a bogey 47 centimetres in diameter.'

'You could just carry on anyway until you get there,' suggested Matthew.

'No point now,' grumbled Danny. 'Natalie used the bogey to play fetch with next door's dog and, instead of bringing it back, he ate it.'

'Gross! I'm surprised your sister wanted to touch the bogey in the first place.'

'She thought it was a rubber ball.' Danny grinned. 'She spent all afternoon washing her hands when she found out what it *really* was! Come on, let's go and beat the Snickwell Alleycats.'

With the studs on their boots clicking an upbeat

rhythm on the floor, Danny's team, the Coalclough Sparrows, walked out of the changing rooms to do just that, by four goals to nil.

'Well done, Danny,' said his dad when they got home from the game. 'You haven't let a goal in all season. If you carry on like this you're going to be better than I was.'

'I doubt it, Dad!'

Danny looked around at the shelves and glass display cabinets crammed with medals, trophies

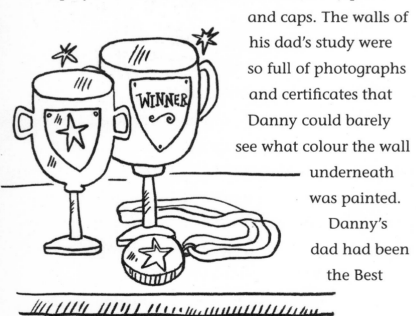

and caps. The walls of his dad's study were so full of photographs and certificates that Danny could barely see what colour the wall underneath was painted. Danny's dad had been the Best

Goalkeeper in
the World Ever.
He played more
times for his
country, won
more medals,
played
in more
games
and let
in fewer goals than
anyone else had ever
done in the history
of football. He even
had a Special Certificate from the Great Big Book of
World Records.

Best Goalkeeper
in the World Ever

WON
THE
CUP!

HE DID
IT AGAIN

SAVE!

100 GOALS
SAVED
BOBBY BAKER!

Hero!

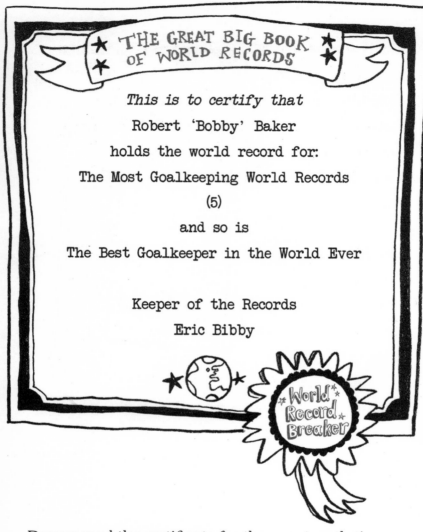

THE GREAT BIG BOOK OF WORLD RECORDS

*This is to certify that*
Robert 'Bobby' Baker
holds the world record for:
The Most Goalkeeping World Records
(5)
and so is
The Best Goalkeeper in the World Ever

Keeper of the Records
Eric Bibby

World Record Breaker

Danny read the certificate for the umpteenth time.
'One day I'll be the best in the world at something,
Dad, just like you.'

His dad smiled. 'You're the best in the world to me, Danny,' he said.

That's not the same, thought Danny. He scratched his head vigorously. Time to try for my next record attempt.

# Nits

Dear Mr Bibby

Last night my mum found 109 head lice on my head. Is this a record? When they checked, my mum and dad had them too. And my sister Natalie discovered that she was simply crawling with nits! She wasn't pleased, because she was just about to go to the school disco with her best friends Kaylie and Kylie.

a nit

natalie

We managed to collect fifty-seven more head lice, making a total of 166.
I have stuck them all on the bottom of this page as proof. Could this be a family record?

I hope it is, because it might make Nats feel better to know that she didn't miss the disco for nothing.

And she might stop trying to pull my ears off every time she sees me.

Yours sincerely
Danny Baker

THE
*GREAT*
* BIG *
*BOOK OF*
* WORLD *
RECORDS

ARE YOU A RECORD
BREAKER ?

Dear Danny Baker

Thank you for the enquiry about your attempt
on the Most Head-lice world record, which I'm
sorry to tell you was unsuccessful.

This record is held by Arthur Grimley, a hermit
from Thornton Watlass in Yorkshire. He lived
alone in a cave on the North Yorkshire Moors
for forty-one years, and never washed in all
that time. His hair and beard reached down to
just above his knees. Whenever ramblers went
near his cave, he used to shout rude words at
them and jump up and down pulling faces. If
this didn't scare them away, he used to pull
his pants down and show them his bottom. I
imagine he had the dirtiest bottom in the world
too, but as far as I know no one dared to check!

One day, Arthur slipped on some ice outside his cave, and luckily was found soon after by some ramblers. He went to hospital and was washed and deloused. They counted 8,433 head lice, as well as 169 fleas. (This isn't a record. The most fleas ever counted on one person is 17,325.)

The record number of head lice ever collected from one family is 58,971. This record is held by the fifteen members of the Pickle family of West Virginia, USA.

Bad luck once again. Perhaps you should buy your sister a present and say you are sorry. Or buy yourself a hat with earmuffs. Sisters are just no fun are they?

Best wishes
Eric Bibby
Keeper of the
Records

The Pickle family W. Virginia

Danny lay in bed that morning, reading Mr Bibby's letter. He sighed with disappointment.

'Danny!' shouted his mum from downstairs. 'Get up, now!'

He got out of bed, yawned, stretched and scratched his tummy. He was wearing socks and trainers, and a pair of extremely grubby underpants. Danny had been wearing the same pants for six months, but so far his mum hadn't realized, because he'd been putting a clean pair in the wash bin every day.

He'd been doing the same with his socks.

Natalie appeared at his open bedroom door and stared at him with a strange mixture of triumph and disgust on her face.

'I'm telling Mum,' she sneered.

'Aw, don't, Nat,' begged Danny. 'She'll go ballistic.'

'You're revolting.'

'I'm just trying to break a world record.'

Natalie pulled a face. 'Which one? The Dirtiest Underpants?'

'No,' replied Danny truthfully, although he realized that he *could* try for that record, if he didn't break the one he was *actually* going for. 'It's a secret.'

'Fine, don't tell me then.' Natalie smirked. 'Mum!'

Danny quickly pulled on his jeans. 'I'll tidy your bedroom,' he offered desperately.

Natalie considered this for a moment, but then yelled, 'Mum!' again.

'I'll ask Matthew to do your maths homework for the next two weeks.'

'*Mum!*'

'What do you want, Natalie?' shouted Mum from downstairs. 'I've got the vacuum cleaner in pieces on the living-room floor.'

Danny pleaded with his eyes.

'Have you seen –' yelled Natalie. She grinned at her brother – 'my hairbrush?'

'No, I haven't,' answered Mum. 'Your bedroom's such a mess, I'm not surprised you've lost it.'

'It'll be tidy by tonight, don't worry.' Natalie glared menacingly at her brother. 'Won't it, Danny?'

'I promise. I'll do it after the game this afternoon.'

'And I won't have to do any maths homework for two weeks?'

'No.'

'OK then.' She stuck her tongue out at him, and went downstairs.

Danny sighed with relief and finished getting dressed. He picked up his football-kit bag and set off for school. The Coalclough Sparrows were going to play Crawshaw Cougars in the semi-final of the Penleydale Schools Cup.

Danny had another great game in goal, and the Sparrows won two–nil.

'We're in the Final!' cried Matthew, rubbing his hair dry with a large Walchester United towel. He and

Danny were getting changed after the match. 'It's fantastic!'

'Who do you think we'll play?' asked Danny. He hadn't had a shower, and was already dressed.

'It doesn't matter. We're playing so well, we can beat anybody.' Matthew threw the towel into his bag. 'Dan, why don't you ever have a shower after a game? Are you trying to break another record?'

'Yeah,' answered Danny, 'I've got a couple of things brewing actually. I didn't realize breaking world records would be so difficult. My Head-lice record attempt didn't even come close.'

'So *you're* the one who's given everyone nits.'

'Yeah.' Danny smiled proudly. 'It was me.'

'What's this new record you're working on then?'

'I'm going to try for the Spottiest Bum in the world. I've not washed my bum or changed my underpants now for nearly six months. That's why I never have a shower after a game.'

'*Six months?*' gasped Matthew. 'Gross!'

'Yeah, it's going really well – my bum is covered

in spots. I'm going to have to count them soon and write to Mr Bibby at the Great Big Book of World Records, because it really hurts when I sit down.'

'I'll bet it does,' said Matthew. 'How are you going to count them?'

Danny tried to look at his bottom over his shoulder, and then bent over to peer at it between his legs. 'I'm not sure. Use a mirror, I suppose. No, wait – you're ace at maths! Why don't you count them for me?'

'No way!'

'That reminds me. Nat the Brat was going to snitch about my underpants. I promised you'd do her maths homework for the next two weeks if she kept her mouth shut. Will you?'

Matthew rolled his eyes. 'Yeah, go on then. But I bet it'll be the first time Nat the Numbskull ever gets ten out of ten for her maths homework.'

'Thanks, Matt. By the way, I'm working on another record attempt too, just in case my spotty bum isn't a world-beater.'

'What?'

'I'm going for the Smelliest Feet record.'

Matthew stared at Danny's feet. 'Cool. How are you going to do it?'

'I've not changed my socks for six months.'

'Double-gross! That's a hundred and eighty days! I put on a clean pair every day!'

Danny beamed. 'I know – great, isn't it! And for the last six weeks I've not taken my shoes off except to put my football boots on.'

'Triple-gross! Not even at night, in bed?' asked Matthew.

'No,' replied Danny. 'If my mum finds out she'll go mad. I sit toasting my toes in front of the fire as much as I can. The rest of the time I keep my feet wrapped in a blanket.'

'They must be *really* sweaty by now,' said

Matthew. Danny could see he was impressed.

'But not sweaty enough,' said Danny. 'When people can smell them with my shoes on, that's when they'll be ready.'

Matthew leaned over Danny's feet and sniffed.

'Not yet,' he said.

'No, not yet,' agreed Danny.

# Spot on the Bot

Dear Mr Bibby

It's me again. I have got 207 spots on my bottom. Is this a record? I've sent a photograph of my bottom as proof. My best friend, Matthew, who took the photo, says it's the most awesome thing he's ever

207 spots (my bum)

seen. To get my bottom in this state, I didn't take off my underpants for over six months. I would have gone on longer, but my underpants had turned green and there     were five small mushrooms growing on them. I was going to donate my pants to

my underpants

the local museum, but when Mum found them, she said they were a health hazard and threw them in the bin.

My bottom hurts and I can't sit down. Please tell me I have broken the record.

Yours sincerely
Danny Baker

PS My football team beat Whelley St Peter's five-nil on Saturday. We've won the league! We've also got the Penleydale Cup Final coming up. I'm the goalkeeper.

PPS My dad is Bobby Baker. He's got a certificate from you, for being the Best Goalkeeper in the World Ever.

The Great Big Book
of World Records
London

ARE YOU A RECORD
BREAKER ?

Dear Danny

207 spots on one bottom is a fantastic
attempt. However, I'm afraid your bottom
is not a world-beater. The Spottiest Bottom
in the World belongs to Thelma McCurdie of
Kissimmee, Florida, USA. On 4 December 1993,
a doctor appointed by the Great Big Book
of World Records counted 11,319 spots on her
bottom. Thelma also holds the record for the
Biggest Bottom in the world. She
has a bottom that an
elephant would be
proud to own, measuring
a humongous 622 cm
in diameter. I have
included a photograph so
that you know what you
are up against.

Thelma's bottom ↑

I hope you can sit down now. If not, why don't
you try to break one of the silliest world
records in the Great Big Book, and one of my
favourites: Leaning Casually Against a Goalpost
While Dressed as a Ponsonby Pork Pie (two years,
five months, sixteen days, nine hours, five
minutes, and fifty-nine seconds)?

Congratulations on winning the league and good
luck in the Cup Final, Danny. You must be very
proud to be the son of Bobby Baker. He was a
great player.

Best wishes
Eric Bibby
Keeper of the Records

Danny and Matthew sat on the kerb outside
Danny's house, reading Mr Bibby's letter.

'You can't try for the Leaning
Casually Against a Goalpost
While Dressed as a Ponsonby
Pork Pie world record,' complained
Matthew. 'You wouldn't be able to
dive on the ground to save a shot,
and we'd lose every match.'

Danny sighed. 'I know. It's tempting though.'

'You can't, Danny,' pleaded Matthew. 'At least,
don't attempt it next Saturday – it's the Cup Final
and Hogton Growlers are a really good side.'

'Don't worry,' said Danny. 'I want to win the Cup
as much as anyone.'

At that moment, he saw his sister heading
towards them, and she didn't look happy.

'You're fish food, Matthew Mason!'
shrieked Natalie. She stormed down the
street, her face as red as a ripe tomato
with sunburn. 'I've got two-weeks'
detention because of you!'

Matthew looked puzzled. 'Did I get your maths homework wrong?'

'No, you dope!' yelled Natalie. 'You got it right!'

'Er . . . that's good, isn't it?' suggested Matthew.

'No, it's not!' shouted Natalie. 'It was *too* right. My maths teacher knew I hadn't done it! Next time you do my homework, get a couple wrong!' She stomped into the house and slammed the front door shut.

Danny looked like he had just got the best birthday present ever.

Matthew looked like a bad smell had just gone up his nose.

It *had*.

He sniffed the air. 'Can you smell gas?' he asked.

'Can *you*?' asked Danny.

'Yeah. I can smell something really rotten, like boiled cabbage and seaweed and eggs and cheese and drains all mixed together.'

Matthew looked around him, trying to find where the awful pong was coming from. His gaze stopped at Danny's feet.

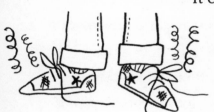

'It can't be,' he said.

'It is!' said Danny. 'They're ready!'

'When are you going to let them out?'

'On Monday in assembly. Take my advice: put a peg on your nose.'

# Pong

Dear Mr Bibby

This must be a record! To get myself ready for this attempt, I've been wearing the same pair of socks and shoes every minute of the day and night for the last few months (except when I played football, then I put football socks over the ordinary ones and wore my football boots).

Yesterday I finally took off my shoes during morning assembly. In just under ten seconds, 201 children, five teachers and Mr Rogers the headmaster were unconscious. Nine children and one teacher escaped the pong, because they had very bad colds and their noses were full of snot. My best friend, Matthew Mason, was all right, because I told him to put a peg on his nose. I did the same.

The teacher who escaped called 999.
Firefighters in protective suits and
breathing masks tried to pull my
socks off, but they couldn't do
it. They took me to hospital,
where my socks were cut away
with special surgical scissors. Two
doctors and a nurse passed out. This makes a
total of 210 people who were knocked out by my
smelly feet.

Whiffy sock

Thirty-three of the children who smelt my
feet are still in hospital. The school still stinks
of boiled cabbage and seaweed and eggs and
cheese and drains all mixed together. My feet
look like two pizzas on the end of my legs, and
they smell a bit like pizzas too!

I really hope this is a record, because I am in
Very Big Trouble. The whole football team's out
of action, except for me and Matthew, and
it's the Cup Final on Saturday. So we're going

to have to play Hogton Growlers with the nine snotty children who survived my feet. Six of the survivors are girls, none of them even likes football, never mind plays it, and all nine have colds! Four of my new teammates are in Year 1! To top it all, my feet are so sore I can't move properly. We're going to get slaughtered.

Do I have the Smelliest Feet in the world? Please say I do, then at least it will have all been worth it.

Yours sincerely
Danny Baker

PS Here is a photograph of me being taken out of school by the firemen.

(me, going to hospital

The Great Big Book
of World Records
London

Dear Danny

ARE YOU A RECORD
BREAKER ?

What a *fantastic* effort! I have checked our
records and you are *almost* a record breaker,
but not quite.

The world record for the Smelliest Feet belongs
to Wilma Wallace of Wagga Wagga, Australia. In
December 1987, after a long day of Christmas
shopping in a shopping mall in Sydney, she
kicked off her shoes in the food hall. 217
people were gassed and had to be taken to
hospital. This only just beats the 210 people
affected by *your* feet. Unfortunately, Wilma was
not actually trying to break the world record
so had not taken the precautions you had. She
did not put a peg on her nose. Sadly, Wilma
was killed by her own feet. She was buried in

a lead-lined coffin. To this day, no grass or flowers will grow on her grave, because her feet still pollute the soil.

This terrible story goes to show, once again, how careful you must be when you try to break a world record.

I hope the Cup Final goes better than you expect it to. If not, remember that it could be worse: just think of Wilma Wallace of Wagga Wagga!

Good luck
Eric Bibby
Keeper of the Records

Danny was more fed  up than he had ever been in his life. It was the morning of the Final, and he was sat in the kitchen swishing his feet in a bowl of warm water.

Matthew knocked on the back door. 'Is it all right to come in?' he asked, glancing warily at Danny's feet.

'Yeah, they still whiff a bit, but they're not dangerous any more,' replied Danny. 'And we don't have to wear pegs on our noses.'

'How do they feel?' asked Matthew.

'Not bad,' replied Danny. He lifted his feet out of the bowl and began to dab them gently them with a towel. 'I have to bathe them three times a day, but they're still sore. The water in the bowl hasn't gone green for the last two days, and the nurse says that's a good sign. I'm not sure though. I left the bowl in the garden yesterday. Two sparrows took a bath in it and all their tail feathers dropped off!'

'Will you be all right to play today?'

Danny sighed. 'I have to, Matt, but I'm not sure I'll be able to get through the whole game.'

Just then they heard Natalie clomping down the stairs.

'Quick,' whispered Danny, 'Nat's coming. Put the peg on your nose.'

'Why?' asked Matthew as he grabbed a wooden clothes peg from the kitchen table, and pinched it on to the end of his nose.

'Because I haven't let on that she doesn't need it any more,' answered Danny, picking up a peg. 'It's too much fun listening to her speak. And when she eats – *gross*!'

Natalie stomped into the kitchen to get her breakfast, and glared at the boys, but with the peg on her nose, she just looked silly, not scary.

Danny and Matthew giggled.

'Bot's so fuddy?' growled Natalie. She slammed the fridge door shut, and flounced out of the kitchen with her bowl of cornflakes.

The boys collapsed in a fit of laughter.

Outside in the car, Dad sounded the horn to hurry them up.

'Time to go,' said Danny.

In the changing room at Penleydale Town FC, Danny pulled his football boots carefully over his sore feet and laced them up. 'Owww,' he moaned as pain shot through his swollen, tender toes.

The referee opened the door and shouted, 'Teams out on the field, please.'

Danny and Matthew looked at

their emergency teammates. The six girls came out from behind a screen at one end of the room, where they had been getting changed. They were giggling.

'These boots are great for tap-dancing,' said Emily Barnes, starting to do a routine in front of the showers.

'They're not taking this seriously, are they?' complained Matthew.

Three of the five-year-olds were kicking a ball to each other. They kept taking huge swings at the ball and missing by a mile.

Danny's shoulders sagged and he frowned at Matthew. 'We don't stand a chance. This is all my fault.'

'You never know, one of the girls might turn out to be the new Pelé,' said Matthew hopefully.

Danny sat down dejectedly on a bench, his head

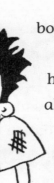

bowed. 'Yeah, right.'

Matthew put his hand on his friend's shoulder. 'There's always next season.'

The Sparrows lined up in the tunnel next to the Hogton Growlers team. Hogton were a big side. They looked at Danny and Matthew, and then at the girls, and then at the little ones at the back, and *then* burst out laughing.

'They should just give us the cup now and save time,' chuckled the Hogton captain.

This is going to be the longest hour of my life, thought Danny.

He hobbled on to the pitch, took up his position in goal and got ready to start the game.

# What a Save!

## PENLEYDALE SCHOOLS CUP FINAL

Penleydale Schools Cup Final

at

Penleydale Town FC

Three Hills Stadium

Coalclough Sparrows v Hogton Growlers

Sponsored by: Crumbly Crunch Biscuits

TEAMS

**Coalclough Sparrows:**

1. Danny Baker [Goalkeeper]
2. ~~Jake Dimbleby~~ AMY JOHNSON
3. ~~Tom O'Brian~~ GRACIE GREEN
4. ~~Josh Davis~~ HARRY HOOD
5. Matthew Mason [Captain]

6. ~~James Sedgley~~ KATIE SEDGLEY
7. ~~Jack Dawkins~~ LILY RUSHTON
8. ~~Harry Warburton~~ SOPHIE RUSHTON
9. ~~Sarwit Chudda~~ EMILY BARNES
10. ~~Sam Walters~~ OLIVER HALL
11. ~~Amir Quaiyoom~~ JACK GORDON
12. ~~Ben Prendergast~~ JAMIE LEE

**Hogton Growlers:**

1. Peter S. Michael [Goalkeeper]

2. Terry Henry

3. Frank Lampoon

4. Steven Gerald

5. Robbie Charlton

6. Paul Schools

7. Kieran Keegan

8. Christian Ronald-Howe

9. David Peckham [Captain]

10. Wayne Mooney

11. Ryan Biggs

12. Alfie Shearer

Hogton kicked off, and in three passes were in Danny's penalty area. The big striker, Wayne Mooney, blasted a fierce shot towards the top corner of the goal.

Danny's smelly feet screamed in agony as he pushed off the ground, but he managed to get his fingertips to the ball and push it over the crossbar.

'Great save, Danny!' shouted Matthew.

From the corner, David Peckham headed the ball down to Danny's left. Danny dropped, and held the ball on the line. The crowd cheered another great save.

The first half went on in exactly the same way: the

Growlers attacking, and Danny making save after save to keep them out. The Hogton goalkeeper didn't touch the ball once in the whole first half.

The referee blew the whistle for half-time. Nil–nil!

Danny got into the changing room and almost collapsed into his seat. He was exhausted.

'Did we win?' asked Amy Johnson.

Matthew ignored her. 'Right, Danny, here's the plan. If you carry on saving everything in the second half, then I'd say there's about a sixteen per cent chance we can win the match on penalties.'

Danny's toxic toes throbbed with pain.

'I can't, Matt. I can't do that again.'

Just then there was a knock at the changing-room door and Danny's dad came in. 'How are your feet?' he asked.

'Terrible,' replied Danny. 'I don't think I'm going to be much use in the second half.'

'Well, whatever happens, I just

43

wanted you to know that your performance in the first half was the best I've ever seen.'

'Really?'

'Danny, you were fantastic – I couldn't have saved some of those shots. I'm really proud of you.'

'Thanks, Dad.'

Danny didn't feel the pain in his feet when he walked back out on to the field. He could have been walking on feathers.

# It's All Over . . .

In the second half, there was nothing Mooney, Ronald-Howe and Peckham could do to beat Danny. But with one minute to go, Wayne Mooney, the Growlers' big striker, got through the defence once more.

Danny moved out to meet him.

The lad had tried to dribble round Danny five times already in the game, but every time Danny had dived bravely at his feet, and picked the ball off his toe. This time Wayne lifted his right foot and blasted the ball towards the goal.

It fizzed past Danny and was heading for the top corner when he somehow arched backwards and managed to touch the ball wide of the post for a corner.

The crowd jumped to their feet and roared and clapped this save, the best one of all. Wayne held his head in his hands.

Danny got up and ran to his goal.

'Come on!' he shouted. 'Everyone back!'

The Growlers' coach screamed at his goalkeeper to go up for the corner, and as the winger took the kick, every other player crowded into Coalclough's penalty area, jostling for position.

It was a good corner kick, arching high and fast into the centre of the area. Danny made his decision and charged off his line, as the Hogton goalkeeper raced forward and leaped high to head the ball. Danny dived and stretched and pulled the ball out of the air with both hands. The Hogton keeper headed nothing, and fell to the ground in a heap. Danny landed on his feet, clutching the ball

tightly to his chest.

Once again the crowd cheered.

'Danny! Shoot!' yelled Matthew.

What's he talking about? thought Danny.

And then he saw it: the empty Hogton goal!

Danny took two steps towards the edge of his penalty area, and with the last bit of strength left in his exhausted legs, punted the ball down the pitch as hard and as high and as straight as he could.

'Owwwww!' His feet had finally had enough. Pain burst up his legs and he collapsed on the grass.

For a moment the whole stadium fell silent. Everyone held their breath. All eyes followed the ball as it looped up high over the halfway line, and then began to fall slowly back to earth. It bounced about fifteen metres inside the Hogton half.

Four of the Growlers team began to race as fast as they could up the field.

The referee chased up the field too, glancing at his stopwatch as the seconds ticked down to the final whistle.

With each bounce the ball got lower and slower, and the four defenders got closer. When it crossed into the Hogton penalty area it was rolling, and they were gaining on it quickly.

The ball trickled over the six-yard line.

The referee looked at his watch again and put the whistle to his lips.

'It's not going to make it,' groaned Danny.

The ball dribbled a metre, then half a metre from the line.

One of the Hogton players was nearly there. He lunged desperately, sliding across the grass towards the ball as it reached the goal line. Danny saw him kick the ball clear, and at the same moment the referee blew his whistle for the end of the game.

The Coalclough supporters shouted, 'GOAL!'

The Hogton supporters yelled, 'NO GOAL!'

'Look!' said Danny, pointing down the pitch. The referee was shaking his head and pointing to his watch. 'It didn't make it.'

'We can still win on penalties,' said Matthew.

Danny groaned quietly. Exhaustion and disappointment rolled over him like a wave. He fell back on the ground and closed his eyes. He had nothing left. He didn't even think he could stand up any more, never mind save five penalties.

Danny just wanted to go to sleep. The howling, bellowing crowd seemed to be a long way away down a deep, dark tunnel.

Suddenly, Danny was being lifted off the ground. He struggled to open his eyes, expecting to see the Coalclough Sparrows' trainers putting him on a stretcher, but there were no trainers and there was no stretcher. He was being carried by people from the crowd, and they were smiling and cheering.

Matthew pushed through the crush of legs and bodies.

'What's going on, Matt?' whispered Danny.

'It *was* a goal!' cried his friend. 'Someone took a video of it and showed the referee. Their player cleared it *after* it crossed the line, and *before* the ref blew the whistle!'

'What?' Danny was groggy and confused.

'WE'VE WON THE CUP!' screamed Matthew.

Two of the Coalclough fans lifted Danny on to their shoulders, and the crowd roared. As they carried him around the pitch, people slapped him on the back and clapped and cheered. Even the girls in the team were dancing with excitement.

'*Now* have we won?' asked Amy Johnson.

'I'm not sure,' answered Gracie Green. 'I think so.'

As the throng of people reached the stand, Danny looked for his mum and dad. He saw them hugging each other and jumping up and down. Mum blew Danny a kiss and Dad punched the air.

And there, on a small table on the pitch in front of the stand, glinting in the sunlight, was the Penleydale Schools Cup.

'Ace!' cried Danny.

'Cool,' agreed Matthew.

# Danny Baker - Record Breaker

Dear Mr Bibby

I believe you know my son, Danny Baker. He tells me that he has written to you several times about his world-record attempts.

Yesterday, Danny won the Penleydale Schools Cup single-handedly. I made a video of the game and have enclosed a copy with this letter. During the game Danny made eighty-seven saves that would have been goals for

Hogton Growlers, the opposition team. Is this a record?

Yours sincerely
Robert Baker

PS Danny doesn't know I have sent this, so if he has not broken a record, can you write back to me and not tell him. He would be very disappointed.

The Great Big Book
of World Records
London

ARE YOU A RECORD
BREAKER ?

Dear Danny

Congratulations on winning the Penleydale
Schools Cup! Your dad sent me a video of
the game. It was a thrilling match and your
performance was heroic. What a goal! What
brilliant saves!

I counted that you made eighty-seven saves in
the match. I am thrilled to tell you that this
beats the previous world record of fifty-six
saves, held by Robert 'Bobby' Baker, who I am
sure you would agree was the Best Goalkeeper
in the World Ever. I am delighted to enclose
your certificate to record this amazing
achievement.

Put your poor feet up, Danny, and have a rest.

They, and you, have earned it. You are a record breaker!

Best wishes
Eric Bibby
Keeper of the Records

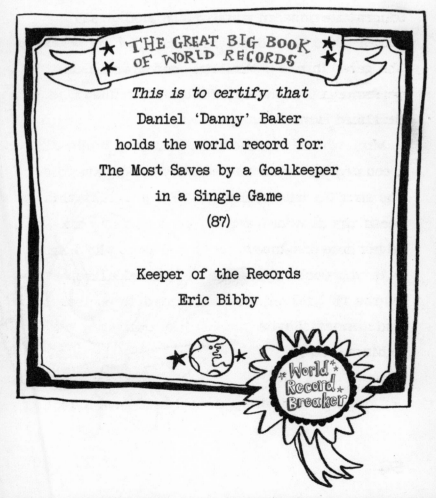

★ THE GREAT BIG BOOK ★
OF WORLD RECORDS

*This is to certify that*
Daniel 'Danny' Baker
holds the world record for:
The Most Saves by a Goalkeeper
in a Single Game
(87)

Keeper of the Records
Eric Bibby

*World Record Breaker*

Danny put the certificate on the wall of his bedroom.

'That's the first of many, Danny,' said his dad. 'Are you going to stop trying to break these silly records and concentrate on what you're really good at: saving goals?'

'Do you think I'll *ever* be as good as you, Dad?'

'You're going to be *better* than me,' replied Dad. He ruffled Danny's hair.

Mum walked into the bedroom with a bright green peg on her nose. 'Wed are you goin' do dell Datalie she doesn' daf do wear a peg od her dose eddybore?'

'Tomorrow,' replied Danny. He held his nose and grinned. 'Baybe.'

Mum laughed. 'Good. Dis ids fud.'

Dad glanced down

at several sheets of writing paper on the bedside table. On the top sheet, Danny had written the words I MUST NOT ATTEMPT TO BREAK WORLD RECORDS IN SCHOOL.

'What's this?' he asked.

'Mr Rogers gave me a hundred lines for letting out my smelly feet in assembly,' explained Danny.

'Ah, well, a hundred's not too many.'

No, thought Danny. A hundred's not enough! There's a record to be broken!

# The Baffled
# Brain Boffins

WARNING!
SHOPPING WITH
MUM CAN DAMAGE
YOUR HEALTH

# Wonderfluff

I must not attempt to break world records in school.
I must not attempt to break world records in school.
I must not attempt to break world records in school.
I must not attempt to break world records in school.
I must not attempt to break world records in school.
I must not attempt to break world records in school.
I must not attempt to break world records in school.
I must not attempt to break world records in school.
I must not attempt to break world records in school.
I must not attempt to break world records in school.
I must not attempt to break world records in school.
I must not attempt to break world records in school.
I must not attempt to break world records in school.
I must not attempt to break world records in school.
I must not attempt to break world records in school.
I must not attempt to break world records in school.
I must not attempt to break world records in school.
I must not attempt to break world records in school.
I must not attempt to bre

To the Keeper of the Records
The Great Big Book of World Records
London

Dear Mr Bibby

Mr Rogers

My headmaster, Mr Rogers, was a bit cross about my attempt to break the Smelliest Feet record. The teachers who had to go to hospital weren't very happy either. The school has been disinfected three times and still stinks of boiled cabbage and seaweed and eggs and cheese and drains all mixed together. Mr Rogers punished me by making me do one hundred lines, but I kept on writing. I did 161½ before he caught me. He got cross about that too, and ordered me do two thousand lines saying I MUST NOT DO MORE LINES THAN THE NUMBER OF LINES I'VE BEEN GIVEN.

I didn't have time to finish them at school, but I kept going at home and managed to do 1,793 before my pen ran out of ink. I'd have done even more, but my sister Natalie caught me

borrowing her Class Prefect pen. She was cross
that I'd tricked her into wearing a peg on her
nose after the smelly feet attempt, and she
told my mum. Then Mum got cross, because I
was supposed to be clearing out the junk under
my bed. No one understands what you have to
give up to be a record breaker.

I've sent all my lines with this letter. Is this a
world record? I hope so, because I'm in trouble
with everyone, except my best friend Matthew.
He understands. And he likes counting the lines
for me.

Yours sincerely
Danny Baker

PS I'm trying to break the Walking Backwards
record, but I keep falling over. My bottom's
purple and green and yellow and black all over
with bruises. Mum said I've got to sit on a big
bag of frozen peas. I've also got massive scabs
on both elbows. Ace!

The Great Big Book
of World Records
London

Dear Danny

Thank you for writing to me again. Your attempt
to break the world record for Punishment
Line Writing fell well short of the mark. You
would have to be incredibly badly behaved to
beat William Archibald Naughtie-McGhie, of
Tillicoultry in Scotland. He was Naughtie by
name, and naughty by nature. William's long
history of naughtiness started when he was
eight years old, but by the time he left school,
he had written a total of 15,201 lines.

Here's how he did it:

He let off a stink bomb in class: 600 lines.
He placed a whoopee cushion on the geography
    teacher's seat: 400 lines.

He hid an enormous furry spider in a bag of
carrots - just as the dinner lady was about
to peel them: 400 lines.

He put paint in the caretaker's mop bucket:
700 lines.

He sprinkled itching powder on the toilet paper
in the girl's washroom: 1,000 lines.

He rearranged all the school library books out
of alphabetical order: 200 lines.

He pulled an ugly face in the class photo:
200 lines.

He glued every chair to the classroom floor:
500 lines.

He wore his clothes back to front, and convinced
the school nurse that his head was on
backwards: 300 lines.

He put cold custard in the teachers' coat
pockets: 500 lines.

He put salt in the sugar shakers, and sugar in
the salt shakers: 400 lines.

He farted in the presence of the Queen during a
royal visit to the school: 5,000 lines.

He blamed the fart on the headmaster:
5,001 lines.

William was grounded for a month for this
last crime, and having to write so many lines
finally made him stop his naughty pranks.
William Archibald Naughtie-McGhie is now grown
up, and is a police inspector in Aberdeen.

I'm sorry to disappoint you, Danny.

Best wishes
Eric Bibby
Keeper of the Records

PS Be careful walking backwards, Danny. The
Persistent Reverse Perambulation record is a
difficult and potentially dangerous one to
break.

Mum pulled her car into a parking
space outside the Wyz Byz
supermarket. Natalie, Danny's
older sister, slid out of the back door
and stood by the car, grumpy and unhappy, with
her arms folded and her shoulders slumped.

Danny climbed out backwards and stumbled
straight into her.

'Mum!' whined Natalie, yanking Danny's ear.
'Tell him to stop treading on my toes!'

'Mum!' complained Danny. 'Tell Nat to stop
pulling my ears off!'

'Behave yourselves, both of you!' snapped Mum.

Natalie got back in the
car. 'I'm staying here,' she
announced. 'It's embarrassing
going anywhere with him
walking backwards all the
time, and dressed like *that*.'
Danny and Matthew had
made a contraption out of a wire
coat hanger, a couple of shin-guards

and the wing mirrors off Dad's old motorbike. It was strapped to Danny's shoulders with a pair of his grandad's braces, so that he could see where he was going in the mirrors when he was walking backwards. He had a cushion strapped tightly to his behind with a bright red and yellow snake belt, to protect his sore bottom.

'I *need* this outfit to help me break the world record for Persistent Reverse Perambulation,' protested Danny.

Mum growled and headed for the supermarket entrance.

As soon as they got inside, Danny backed into the stack of blue baskets by the door.

'Sorry, Mum. I wasn't looking in my mirrors.'

Mum glared at Danny as he bumped into an old lady's shopping trolley.

'I *do* apologize,' said Mum. 'He's trying to break a record.'

'Trying to break his neck, more like,'
grumbled the old lady.

Mum grabbed Danny's
shoulder and guided him down
the aisle.

'Hold on to my trolley,' she
ordered. 'And don't let go.'

Danny did as he was told. Mum threw
a few cans of Spaghetti Footballs into the trolley
and marched off. She was going so
quickly up and down the aisles
that Danny struggled to keep up
with her. They rounded a corner
into the baby-care aisle, and Mum stopped so
suddenly that Danny nearly fell over.

'What on earth . . . ? Danny, look at this!'

Danny peered into his mirrors, and saw
a three-metre high inflatable baby,
wearing a gigantic plastic nappy.

'Ace! That's Baby Ben
Bradshaw of Biggleswade,
the Wonderfluff Nappy Tot

off the TV ads,' said Danny. 'I wonder if that's the
biggest blow-up baby in the world? It could be a
record breaker.'

'Don't start, Danny,' warned Mum.

'Sorry. Can I go down to the magazine section?'
he asked. 'I want to see if me or Dad have got
a mention in the latest issue of *It's a Save! The
Goalkeeper's Monthly*.'

Mum looked doubtful.

'I'll be careful, honest,' promised Danny.

Mum sighed. 'Yes, go on then.'

He took two steps back from the shopping
trolley and crashed into Baby Ben Bradshaw
of Biggleswade. As they collided, and the giant
balloon baby bounced upwards, Danny tried to
grab it without turning
round and ruining
his record attempt,
but he only
managed to push
Baby Ben higher in
the air.

Danny glanced in one of his rear-view mirrors
and watched in horror as . . .

. . . the baby wobbled
gently upwards, and
nudged a mound of toilet
rolls . . .

. . . the mound of
toilet rolls tumbled,
and smashed into
cartons of eggs . . .

. . . the eggs flew – splat! – on to the
Cornflakes . . .

. . . the Cornflakes bashed
the Barleybricks . . .

. . . the Barleybricks
pushed the Brancrisps . . .

. . . the Brancrisps bumped
the Sugardrops . . .

. . . the Sugardrops toppled
a tower
of toffee
tins . . .

. . . the toffee tins rolled into a pyramid of melons . . .

. . . the pyramid collapsed and the melons hurtled like loose bowling balls into rows of fizzy-cola bottles, sending them swirling and whirling and twirling into the air.

'Look out, Mum!' yelled Danny, pushing her behind a display of lemon-puff biscuits.

The plastic cola bottles smacked on to the ground and the fizzy liquid inside was so shaken up that the tops exploded from them like bullets.

By now the Wonderfluff baby had come back down to earth. It lay on its hands and knees with its enormous inflated rump sticking up in the air, being peppered by bottle tops. They made a pleasant drumming sound on the big blow-up nappy, until suddenly there was a loud 'BANG'!

Baby Ben Bradshaw of Biggleswade, the Wonderfluff Nappy Tot, quivered and shuddered. Then, with a huge roaring whistling fart, took off into the air above Danny and his mum.

The jet-propelled baby whistled and swooped around the Wyz Byz store, knocking over more displays and ripping signs from the ceiling.

'Mum!' shrieked Danny as blow-up Baby Ben banked and looped over the frozen-fish cabinet and went fizzing directly towards her.

All thoughts of his record gone, Danny turned around and raced towards his mother. She stood transfixed and terrified as the giant plastic infant charged at her like an angry bull. At that moment Danny's world went into slow motion. His head throbbed with the sound of his own thumping heartbeat and the horrible whine of the monster baby's squealing fart.

The rocketing inflatable skimmed the puff pastry . . . shaved the nose-hair trimmers . . . brushed the cotton-wool balls . . . and closed in on his mum. With one final despairing effort Danny launched himself upwards, his body arching gracefully into the air as though reaching to save a penalty in the top corner of his goal. He stretched and pushed the baby-shaped missile away from his mum and up towards the roof.

The impact smashed Danny into a pile of giant-sized Wonderfluff nappy boxes, and the whole lot crashed down on top of him.

Everything went black.

# Gobbledegook

Danny opened his eyes and looked around. He was in a strange bed, surrounded by flashing, beeping, whirring instruments. There was a woman nearby dressed in a pale blue uniform, with white clogs on her feet.

She was writing in a file of papers.

Danny guessed that he was in hospital.

He was tremendously thirsty and asked the nurse for a glass of water. 'My cardigan is full of holes, earwax,' he croaked.

The nurse looked up from the papers. 'You're awake.' She smiled.

'Gumboots, Bobbin,' replied Danny.

The nurse frowned.

'How do you feel, young man?'

Danny licked his parched lips and tried to ask

again for a drink. 'My cardigan is full of holes, earwax,' he repeated.

'Is it?' answered the nurse. She looked puzzled. 'You were bumped on the head by a giant box of Wonderfluff nappies. Do you have a headache?'

Danny shook his head. 'Beep, Bobbin,' he replied. 'But the blue kangaroo is tired and my cardigan *is* full of holes.'

'Er . . . of course it is,' said the nurse, and scurried out of the room.

She returned a minute later accompanied by a small, smiling doctor.

'Hello, Danny.'

Danny held his hand up in greeting. 'Bucket scoops, Wobble,' he replied.

The doctor raised his eyebrows.

'My name's Doctor Gururangan, but you can call me Doctor Sri. How are you feeling?'

Danny mimed drinking, and said, 'My cardigan is full of holes.'

'Would you like a glass of water?' asked Dr Sri, filling one from a nearby jug.

'Gumboots, earwax!' exclaimed Danny.

He gulped the water thirstily. 'Saddlebags,' he said as he rubbed his mouth with the back of his hand.

Dr Sri flashed a light into each of Danny's eyes. 'Do you remember what happened to you?' he asked.

'Gumboots, Wobble,' answered Danny, nodding. 'The blob pickled the plum basket and the treetops threw pies at a wombat.'

The doctor and nurse glanced at each other.

'I've never seen anything like this before,' admitted Dr Sri.

He picked up the red telephone and pressed four numbers. After a moment he said, 'Professor Walkinshaw, would you come down straight away and examine Danny Baker? I know it's very rare, but I think we may have a case of Trauma-induced Nonsensical Pronouncements.'

When the professor ambled into the room, he

wasn't at all what Danny was expecting. He had untidy hair and long, curly mutton-chop whiskers. Under his crumpled white coat he wore an old tartan shirt, baggy blue trousers and cowboy boots. For some reason, Professor Walkinshaw reminded Danny of his grandad's favourite comfy old chair.

'Hi, Danny.'

'Bucket scoops, Wobble.'

'How are you doing, young man?'

'My ears can see daisies.'

'Interesting,' murmured the professor. He turned to the nurse. 'Have you had *any* sense from Danny?'

'None, Professor. He's been talking complete gobbledegook since he woke up.'

The professor rubbed his chin. 'This *can* happen when patients wake in a strange place. Danny might begin to talk normally when he sees something familiar.'

'Danny's family and his best friend Matthew Mason are waiting outside,' suggested the nurse.

'OK, show them in and let's give it a try,' said
Professor Walkinshaw.

Danny's mum raced in and kissed and hugged
Danny tightly. His dad ruffled Danny's hair.

'Bucket scoops, Beans on Toast,' said
Danny. He smiled at Natalie.
'Bucket scoops, Dopey.'

Matthew stood by the
door and gave him the
thumbs up.

Danny grinned at his
best friend. 'Wonderfluff!'

Mum frowned. 'Danny,
what are you talking about?'

'Snowflakes burnt my banjo, Beans!'

Mum and Dad looked at each other anxiously,
and then at the doctors. 'We don't understand.
What's the matter with him?'

'I'm afraid Danny has a severe case of Trauma-
induced Nonsensical Pronouncements,' answered
the professor.

Dr Sri smiled at Danny's mum and dad. 'What

the professor means is that the blow on the head has made Danny talk gibberish.'

Natalie snorted. 'Danny always talks gibberish – how can you tell the difference?'

'Dribble on the fat bucket, Dopey,' replied her brother.

'I was hoping that it was a mere case of Temporary Acute Vocabulary Disorientation Syndrome,' said the professor. 'But obviously it's more serious than that.'

'Unfortunately, seeing your familiar faces hasn't cured him,' explained Dr Sri. 'But don't worry, if anyone can make Danny well again, it's Professor Walkinshaw. He's the world's leading expert on baffling illnesses.'

'Nothing's beaten me so far,' confirmed the professor.

'So he will get better?' asked Mum.

'I hope so, Mrs Baker, but I can't promise. You may never understand another word Danny says to you, ever again.'

'Tootle on the turtle, Bernard?' asked Danny.

'Yeah, I'm OK, Dan,' replied Matthew. 'How're you?'

'Our tadpole licks a carrot. Are your drumsticks marching up my nose?'

Matthew rummaged in his pocket and pulled out a half-eaten bar of chocolate. 'This is all I've got,' he said, 'but you can have it if you want.'

'Wonderfluff!'

'Just a minute,' interrupted Professor Walkinshaw, gazing at Matthew. 'Can you understand what Danny is saying?'

'Yeah, course I can,' answered Matthew. 'He just said he was starving and did I have anything nice to eat.'

Danny nodded and looked at his mum. 'The worms are cooking tea cosies in the cup.'

Matthew laughed. 'He said he's glad the giant farting baby didn't hurt you.'

'So what did he mean by "Dribble on the fat

bucket, Dopey"?' asked Natalie.

Matthew glanced cheekily at Danny. 'Er . . . he said that you're looking extremely beautiful today, Natalie.'

The boys sniggered. Natalie glared at them.

'This is even more baffling,' said the professor. 'The *Extraordinary Understanding* of Trauma-induced Nonsensical Pronouncements is even rarer than Trauma-induced Nonsensical Pronouncements itself.'

Matthew looked at Danny and rolled his eyes. 'You're a trillion times easier to understand than *him*,' he said.

'Wonderfluff!' laughed Danny.

'Cool!' agreed Matthew.

# The Baffling Children

St Egbert's Children's Hospital, Walchester

Bucket scoops, Captain Barnacle

All's well now bouncing Bernard can whistle at
a box of toenails. She's a lid off a daffodil with
trumpets, but she's got loops on a drainpipe
to hoot! Sticky-tape buns climbed a feathery
broom for bits and bobs of Ace delight, but
fairies strum the droop.

Hey diddle diddle, Bernard winks merrily at the
dishcloths of doom.

My wobbles die happy. The widgets swoon and
Bernard can swing my trainers to fly through
the ears of camels. Doggies sing for droopy
drawers! Wonderfluff!

Can three coughing spacemen drip whiskers on the Fingers of Gloop? The petals cut through the beans and juggled with a pair of buttery bats, then prancing angels dazzled the piles of withering toads, daring the pots to swish their mangles: purple hippos, purple llamas, purple lions or purple elephants. Oink!

What do piglets find so funny, when mummies do the tango?

Ding-dong
Drainy Babbler

Hello, Mr Bibby

My best friend Matthew will translate this
letter for you. I'm writing
gobbledegook at the moment,
and I'm talking gobbledegook as
well. I was hit on the head by
a great big box of Wonderfluff
nappies, and now I keep talking
rubbish.

The weird thing is, Matthew can
understand everything I say.

The doctors are baffled. They've asked Matthew
to stay at the hospital too, so that he can
tell them what I'm saying. We're both getting
to miss school! Ace!

Remember how I was trying to break the
record for Walking Backwards? I had to stop
to save my mum from being bashed by a big

HUGE
baby

blow-up baby, but I know exactly how long I walked backwards for, because the accident broke my watch: thirteen days, thirteen hours, thirteen minutes and thirteen seconds.

Spooky!

Did I break the record as well as my watch?

SPOOKY!

Best wishes
Danny Baker

ARE YOU A RECORD
BREAKER ?

'Bucket scoops', Danny and Matthew

I'm sorry to hear about your accident with
the box of nappies, Danny, but I'm glad to see
your illness hasn't affected your interest in
breaking records.

The World Record for Persistent Reverse
Perambulation is held by Billy Walklater of
Ambleside, Cumbria. He took walking backwards
into the twenty-first century when he began
using satellite navigation to guide him along.
Unfortunately, after 332 days of Reverse
Perambulation, his satnav took him down a dead
end, and he walked backwards into a brick wall.

Billy had broken the record, but his attempt was over. So he decided to make the most of the situation and go for the world record for Standing Against a Brick Wall. He has been there for 421 days so far, but has another 2965 days to go to before he can claim that record.

Get well soon, Danny!

Ding-dong
Eric Bibby
Keeper of the Records

Professor Walkinshaw and Dr Sri stood by Danny's bed.

'Danny, I've contacted my fellow Brain Boffins around the world to tell them about you, and they're *very* excited. You and Matthew are unique, and they all want to meet you.'

'Snip-snap,' remarked Danny.

'That's nice,' said Matthew.

'I'd like you both to spend a few days on the Bertha Blenkinsop Ward, so that we can study you and try to make you better, Danny.'

'It's where all the other children with baffling illnesses stay.' Dr Sri smiled. 'It's got a really good games room.'

**Bertha Blenkinsop Ward**

'Helping those with baffling illnesses...'

'Wonderfluff!' said Danny. 'Clean that tricky zebra and keep the garden small.'

'Yeah,' agreed Matthew. 'Let's hope there *are* some kids our age to play with.'

At the door to the ward, Dr Sri stopped and pulled a false beard out of his pocket. It was short

and black. He hooked the ends over his ears, and carefully arranged the beard close to his chin.

He reached into a small box by the door, and pulled out two more beards. He handed a long, curly orange one to Danny, and a thick, bushy brown one to Matthew.

'Will you put these on, please?' he said.

'Why?' asked Matthew.

Dr Sri smiled. 'You'll see.'

He led them down the corridor towards three nurses who were standing by the reception desk. They were wearing false beards too. One of them strolled over to the boys.

'I'm Sister Morris,' she said,

'and you must be Danny and Matthew.'

She showed them into the games room, where a boy and girl sat in front of a screen, using handsets to control two brightly coloured racing cars speeding around a track. The boy was also wearing a false beard.

'Bucket scoops!' called Danny.

'That means "Hello",' said Matthew. 'Danny's started to talk gobbledegook, and only I can understand him. That's why we're here. I'm Matthew, by the way.'

'Hi, my name's Alex,' said the boy, 'and this is Abigail.'

'What time's the doorknob?' asked Danny.

'What's wrong with you?' translated Matthew.

'Well, my bottom turns blue whenever I eat a banana,' replied Alex.

'And my ears began to buzz when my dad grew

a beard,' said Abigail. 'Listen.'

Danny and Matthew leaned close to Abigail. Her ears were buzzing softly, as if each one had a small bee trapped inside it.

'Wonderfluff!' breathed Danny.

'Cool,' agreed Matthew. 'Why aren't *you* wearing a false beard?' he asked Abigail.

'Because I'm the reason everyone's wearing them in the first place,' she explained. 'Professor Walkinshaw is hoping I'll be cured if I get used to the sight of them.'

'Has it worked?' asked Matthew.

'It's starting to,' answered Abigail. She reached for a small square black box that hung around her neck on a strip of pink ribbon. 'This is a sound-level meter. The reading's getting lower and lower all the time. You should have heard the noise when it began. My ears sounded like racing cars!'

Danny laughed. 'Wonderfluff!' His tummy rumbled. 'Why did you shovel coal on a mongoose?' he asked. 'Cream crackers!'

Alex and Abigail looked at Matthew.

'That means, "When do we have lunch? I'm starving!"'

'In about half an hour,' replied Alex. 'But don't get excited, the food here *stinks*. You're lucky it's not Friday, or you'd be getting stinky fish.'

'Yeah, *and* beans and sprouts and cabbage,' complained Abigail.

Matthew pulled a face. 'Gross.'

'It's great fuel for farts though,' commented Alex. 'On Fridays we can all trump for England.'

Danny's eyes lit up as an idea popped into his head.

'Tip-tap the moonbeams, because kittens bob their heads to tubas,' he said.

Matthew frowned. 'What are you up to, Danny?'

Alex and Abigail looked puzzled.

'What did he say?' asked Alex.

'This Friday, every kid in the hospital must hang on to their trumps,' explained Matthew.

'Why?' giggled Abigail.

'Walnuts are skating down the rug because their noses are like train sets,' babbled Danny. 'Snooker cue.'

Matthew grinned. 'We're going to try and break the world record for the Loudest Trump – pass it on.'

'How do we dollop cat-food on the light bulbs of smooth?!' Danny asked.

 Alex and Abigail turned to Matthew. 'Why trump for England when we can trump for the world?!'

# Shock Tactics

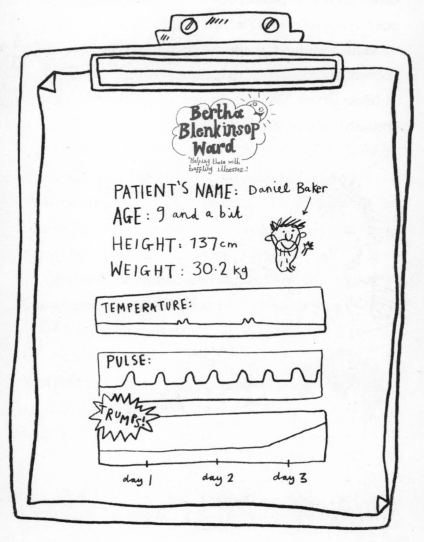

Danny yawned, stretched and trumped. Alex and Abigail were right: this horrible hospital food was *brilliant* fart fuel. Matthew had been running tests with the sound-level meter, trying to see which food produced the loudest trumps. He'd calculated that boiled cabbage produced the most gas and the longest trumps, beans gave the best sound and most pleasant vibrating tone, but sprouts were best for volume.

Over the past few days, a steady stream of Brain Boffins had walked into Danny's room and stood scratching their heads and stroking their false beards in bafflement. They had tried various cures, but so far nothing had worked.

They had talked to Danny in his own style of gobbledegook.

'Tie up the egg roll and fan a broom socket,' said the professor.

'I've tussled with tumbleweed on a damp and dusty bee,' pronounced Dr Sri.

'Flip a goalpost sandwich,' exclaimed Sister Morris.

Danny stared at them. 'Snitch the crumpets, bar none,' he said.

'What a load of rubbish,' translated Matthew.

Danny woke up one morning and there was a huge cardboard cut-out of Baby Ben Bradshaw staring down at him from the end of

his bed. He jumped in fright, but it didn't cure him.

Neither did being tapped
gently on the head for an
hour with a Wonderfluff
nappy.

Danny got out
of bed and put on his
dressing gown. He shuffled sleepily
down the ward towards the games room.
He opened the door and jumped back in shock.

The room was crammed with children, doctors
and nurses. Danny's mum
and dad, and Matthew's
mum and dad were there
too, along with Natalie
and Matthew, Alex and
Abigail. Everyone (apart
from Abigail), was wearing
a false beard, but what
astonished Danny most was
that every single person in the
room was wearing a supersized
Wonderfluff nappy over the

top of their normal clothes.

Danny shook his head as if trying to shake the sight from his eyes.

They all stared back at him, silent and hopeful.

'Well?' asked Mum anxiously.

Danny rolled his eyes. 'Are the watering cans woozy because there's a singing kipper in my trouser pocket?' he asked.

Everyone in the room groaned with disappointment.

Matthew grinned. 'No, Dan, we're not all wearing nappies because we had the hospital curry last night. The Boffins thought the sight of everyone wearing a nappy would cure you.'

Danny glanced at Natalie and chuckled. 'Why smudge Dopey when you can elbow the bursting bubbles?' he asked.

Matthew laughed. 'You're right, Dan, she does look a total twit!'

Natalie's face turned crimson. She ripped her nappy off and hurled it to the floor. 'You are going to be *so* sorry about this!' she growled at the boys

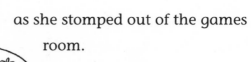

as she stomped out of the games room.

'Nappies off, everyone,' called Dr Sri.

Professor Walkinshaw sighed heavily. 'The Sudden Visual-trigger Sensory-overload Resolution has failed,' he announced. '*I've* failed.'

'This is the most baffling case I've ever seen,' one of the Brain Boffins commented. 'We need more brains on this one.'

The professor nodded thoughtfully. 'I'm going to call every Baffleologist in the world. We'll have a symposium, and Danny and Matthew will be the stars of the show!'

# The Mighty Trump

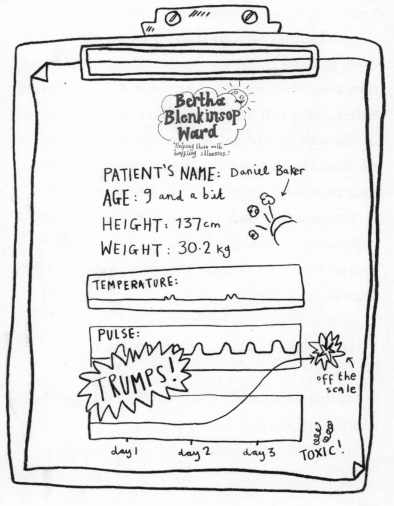

**Bertha Blenkinsop Ward**
*Helping those with baffling illnesses..!*

PATIENT'S NAME: Daniel Baker
AGE: 9 and a bit
HEIGHT: 137cm
WEIGHT: 30.2 kg

TEMPERATURE:

PULSE:

TRUMPS!

off the scale

day 1    day 2    day 3    TOXIC!

Today was the Big Day:
Stinky-fish Friday.

The games room was full
of kids. Matthew had been
round the hospital to pass on
the plan, and everyone who
*could* be there *was* there. Matt had calculated that
they needed at least sixty bottoms. Everybody had
eaten stinky fish and beans and cabbage for lunch,
along with second helpings of sprouts. Alex had
even had third helpings. Their stomachs gurgled
and groaned and grumbled as the gas built up.

Danny and Matthew stood in the
centre of the room.

'Hurry,' moaned Alex. 'I'm going to
explode.'

Danny knew how he felt.

'Did the snapdragon spread jam on a
windmill?'

Matthew looked at Abigail. 'Have you got the
sound-level meter?' he asked.

She nodded and handed the small black box to

Matthew. 'Actually, I don't need it any more,' she admitted. 'My ears stopped buzzing completely yesterday when I saw all those beards. I didn't tell them I was cured though, because they'd have sent me home and I'd have missed the Trump.'

Matthew placed the sound-level meter in the centre of the room.

'Drop a bread bin up the stairs and brush the scooter,' Danny told Matthew. 'Tall tigers wrestle with a jelly flea and watch the pink rabbits "boom!".'

'Everyone bend over and point your bottoms at the meter,' Matthew instructed.

'Danny'll count to three – sorry, I mean "flea" – and when he says "boom!" let rip!'

The kids put their fingers in their ears and bowed low.

Danny shouted, 'Bun . . . glue . . . flea . . . boom!'

As one, they blew out the built-up gas. It was a humongous, growling, roaring trump. It

 was a trump so loud and ferocious that the windows in the room shattered, the television exploded, a water pipe burst, picture frames crashed off the wall,

chairs clattered over, books toppled from bookshelves, the light in the room began to flicker, and everybody's false beards flew off.

'Tickle my flowerpots!' exclaimed Danny.

Professor Walkinshaw and Dr Sri hurried into the room and stared at the devastation.

'What's that terrible smell?' asked Dr Sri, holding his nose.

'Was it a gas leak?'

'Was it an earthquake?' yelled the professor.

'It was a trump,' explained Matthew.

'Something happened to my bottom!' cried Alex, looking shocked.

'And mine!' laughed Matthew, holding his behind and wiggling. 'It was a ripper!'

'No, I mean something else, something . . . *strange*.'

Alex picked up a banana from the floor, where it had been blown out of the fruit bowl by the force of the trump. He peeled it, took a big bite and swallowed. After a moment, he dropped his trousers and glanced over his shoulder. Everyone stared at Alex's bottom, and his bottom stared back at them, pink and rosy. It hadn't turned blue!

The professor was thrilled. 'Heavens to Betsy!'

he exclaimed. 'He's been cured! This is all thanks to you, Danny! Accidental Flatulence-induced Symptom Resolution is unheard of!'

Dr Sri translated, 'He means that this is the first time anyone has been accidentally cured by a trump.'

'Wonderfluff!' exclaimed Danny.

The professor stroked his false beard thoughtfully. 'It could be the loudness or the force of the trump that produced the resolution,' he said. 'But I suspect that the precise mixture of chemicals in the trump gas reacted with the blue in Alex's bottom and turned it pink.'

'We need to analyse it quickly, before it disappears,' said Dr Sri.

Danny's tummy rumbled. 'Peel the flutey bugle, Wobble, and dangle a lollypop!' he laughed.

'Don't worry, Doctor, there's plenty more where that came from!' Matthew translated.

'Bernard, is the octopus melting on the

skateboard?' Danny asked him.

His friend went over to the sound-level meter and looked at the reading. 'We got a hundred and ninteen point nine decibels.'

'The grass-green mole was the pick of the chocolate cans.'

'Yeah, you're right, Danny, that *must* be a record,' agreed Matthew. 'Should we get writing to Mr Bibby?'

'Gumboots!' Danny grinned.

# The Stars of the Show

St Egbert's Children's Hospital, Walchester

Bucket scoops, Captain Barnacle

I'm Drainy boots. Our carpets go moo, and bouncing Bernard rumbles merrily in his coffee-pot, for better or worms.

The lemony handbags pickled on your tram tracks and saw deep wallows of tinkling lilac troops. An aeroplane shook a Snowball, but it wouldn't shake for Drainy. When penguins waddled on woozy tops, lava lamps waltzed on an itchy gumboil and couldn't slurp in a Fusspot. Warty diggers snuggle-up bumps! Did the whatnot rasp a nippy biscuit?

Ding-dong
Drainy Babbler

Hello, Mr Bibby

It's Danny again. I'm still talking nonsense, so my best friend Matthew will tell you what I'm saying, like last time.

Yesterday, sixty-seven of the kids at the hospital produced a trump that measured 119.9 decibels. It cured our new friend Alex, but it didn't cure me. After the damage the trump caused, the hospital says it is never going to serve stinky fish and beans and sprouts and cabbage on a Friday ever again. The kids say I'm a hero! Was our trump a world-beater?

TRUMP!

s-t-i-n-k-y cabbage

Best wishes
Danny Baker

trump

109

The Great Big Book
of World Records
London

ARE YOU A RECORD
BREAKER ?

Dear Danny and Matthew

Bad luck again! You and your friends blew just
short of the record. A couple more sprouts might
have made all the difference.

The Loudest Single Trump ever recorded was
measured at 121.4 decibels. It was produced
by the Woolloomooloo Didgeridoo rugby team
on 14 July 1996 during a tour of Tonga. Like
you, they had been fuelled by a special diet
- stinky fish, spinach, cabbage, pumpkin and
bananas. At a banquet held in their honour, on
a signal from their captain Hayden Blow, the
whole team broke wind simultaneously in front
of King Taufa-ahau Tupou IV.

The team broke the Trump Decibel world record,

but offended the king and his people so much
that they were asked to leave Tonga and never
return.

I hope you put your fingers in your ears when
you trumped. 119.9 decibels is about as loud as
a jet aircraft taking off, but I don't suppose I
need to tell *you* that!

I'm really sorry you're not better yet, Danny,
but don't give up hope, there is *always* a cure.
As your new friend Alex discovered with your
monster trump, the trick is just to find it.

Best wishes
Eric Bibby
Keeper of the Records

Danny stood with Mum, Dad and Matthew outside the Big Hall at the University of Walchester. The room was packed with hundreds of Brain Boffins from all over the world, all there to examine Danny and Matthew.

Dad ruffled Danny's hair.

'How do you feel, Dan?'

'GB.'

Mum put her arm around Danny's shoulders.

'Are you sure? You seem a bit fed up to me.'

Danny shrugged. 'The clock is full of wobbles and custard, Beans,' he explained. 'The cat can smile for ants and a spoon can ring its socks.'

Mum looked at Matthew.

'I don't want to baffle doctors any more, Mum,' Matthew translated. 'It was fun for a while, but now I want to be normal again.'

Inside the hall, Danny heard Professor Walkinshaw announce

to the hundreds of assembled Brain Boffins, 'Ladies and gentlemen, may I introduce the most baffling case I have ever seen: Danny Baker and his best friend Matthew Mason.'

For the next hour Danny and Matthew told their story and answered questions in their uniquely baffling way. At the end of the session the boys walked off the stage to deafening cheers and clapping.

Mum gave Danny a hug.

Dad shook Matthew's hand.

'Well done, both of you,' said Dad.

'It's a bookworm, Toast,' sighed Danny. 'Do dancing spots worry a dinosaur's boots? Because the cows on bicycles have tea-bag toes.'

Matthew frowned and translated, 'I'm a bit fed up, Dad. Do you think I'll ever be able to speak normally again? All I can look forward to are loads more tests.'

Mum knelt down and looked at Danny. She was smiling.

'There *is* something else to look forward to,' she

said. 'I've got some news that will cheer you up.'

'Turnip?' asked Danny.

'What?' asked Matthew.

'I'm going to have a baby,' Mum said.

Danny's jaw dropped. He felt as though his breath had got stuck in his chest. He couldn't get air in or out. He made several choking sounds.

'Danny . . . ?' said Mum anxiously.

Danny tried with all his might to force the air out of his throat. It burst out in a rush of words.

'Whatdoyoumeanyouaregoingtohaveababy?' he blurted.

'What do you mean, you are going to have a baby?' Matthew translated.

'What?' asked Dad.

'What?' asked Mum.

'He said, "What do you mean, you are going to have a baby?"' repeated Matthew.

'I *know* that's what he said!' shouted Mum.

'Danny!' yelled Dad. 'I think you're cured! Say something else.'

'Fidget on a corner flag, Beans on Toast.'

Mum, Dad and Matthew gasped.

Danny laughed. 'Just kidding!'

At that moment, Professor Walkinshaw walked off the stage.

'Danny, Matthew, you've baffled the world of Boffindom,' he beamed. 'But don't worry, I promise we *will* find a cure.'

'It's OK, Professor, I've just had an Out-of-the-blue Mum-delivered Baby-news Gobbledegook Cure,' announced Danny.

The professor frowned. 'What?' he asked.

'His mum's going to have a baby,' Matthew translated. 'And Danny can talk normally again.'

'Ace!' said Danny.

'Don't you mean Wonderfluff?' laughed Matthew.

# Danny Baker - Record Breaker

Dear Mr Bibby

baffled
BRAIN

This is me writing! Guess what? The only person talking gobbledegook now is my doctor, Professor Walkinshaw. He says I've had a 'Resolution by Unexpected Announcement of Impending Sibling Arrival'. In other words, I'm cured!

Just before my mum told me she was going to have a baby, me and Matthew managed to baffle 1,327 Brain Boffins from all over the world. The professor said that in all his years as the world's leading Baffleologist, he'd never known so many big-brained Brain Boffins to be baffled at one time. Does this mean we're world-beaters?

Best wishes
Danny

Dear Danny

This is wonderful news! I was very worried
about you and I am so relieved you are
better. It's also great to hear about your
truly outstanding display of Boffin-baffling.
Congratulations! I can confirm that you and
Matthew have broken the world record for
Tandem Simultaneous Baffling of Big-brained
Brain Boffins.

I have enclosed two certificates, one for each of
you.

Your letter arrived just in time. I leave
today for Lake Chargoggagoggmanchaugga-
goggchaubunagungamaugg, near the town of
Webster, Massachusetts. It has the longest place

name in America, and has more letter 'g's than any other word in the world.

The name of the lake means something like 'Englishmen at Manchaug at the fishing place at the boundary'. The townspeople are hoping to gather at least 2,461 Englishmen at the fishing place at the boundary, to break the previous record. I am going to count how many Englishmen turn up and, as an Englishman myself, take part in the attempt.

With luck, Danny, this time next week, I could be a record breaker too!

Well done to both of you.

Best wishes
Eric Bibby
Keeper of the Records

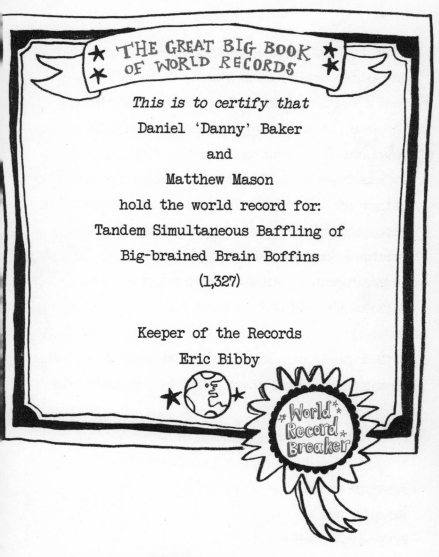

THE GREAT BIG BOOK
OF WORLD RECORDS

*This is to certify that*
Daniel 'Danny' Baker
and
Matthew Mason
hold the world record for:
Tandem Simultaneous Baffling of
Big-brained Brain Boffins
(1,327)

Keeper of the Records
Eric Bibby

World
Record
Breaker

Danny and Matthew stared at their certificates.

'Ace,' said Danny.

'Cool,' agreed Matthew.

Dad ruffled Matthew's hair. 'You deserve that, Matt,' he said. 'Danny would have been in a real pickle without you.'

Mum sat at the kitchen table, fixing the broken toaster. 'So, Danny, would you prefer a brother or a sister?' she asked.

Danny and Matthew looked at each other as if they thought Mum had gone mad.

'A brother, of course!' answered Danny. He nodded towards his sister Natalie. 'One Nasty Nat's enough!'

Natalie put her tongue out at him.

Danny pulled a face at her. Then his eyes widened as a new idea popped into his head.

'I wonder what the world record is for the Stinkiest Nappy?'

# Glossary of Danny Baker's Gobbledegook

Bucket scoops – Hello

Ding-dong – Best wishes

Gumboots – Yes

Beep – No

Earwax – Please

Saddlebags – Thank you

Wobble – Doctor

Bobbin – Nurse

Beans – Mum

Toast – Dad

Bernard – Matthew

Drainy Babbler – Danny Baker

Captain Barnacle – Mr Bibby

Dopey – Natalie

GB – OK

Wonderfluff! – Ace!

# The Pain
# in Spain

# Sick-bags

To the Keeper of the Records
The Great Big Book of World Records
London

Dear Mr Bibby,

I flew to Spain yesterday and I filled thirteen sick-bags on the flight. Mum says it was all the cola and cheese and pickle sandwiches I had at the airport. She's right, they always make me barf. That's why I had them!

Is this even close to breaking the record for filling sick-bags? If it's not, I'll try again on the way home. I can eat some paella. That makes me barf even more!

Best wishes
Danny Baker
(Aged nine and a half)

PS We're here because my dad has been
offered a job as the Manager of Real Marisco.
PPS We're staying at the Hotel La Langosta.
It's posh!
PPPS My best friend Matthew has come too, but
I had to count the sick-bags myself. This time,
Matt wouldn't do the maths!

Dear Danny,

Don't even try for this one! You don't stand
a chance, even if you had cheese and pickle
sandwiches *and* paella!

On a non-stop flight between Paris and Sydney,
Marcel Pompidou of Quimper, France, managed
to fill 144 standard-sized airline sick-bags.
Newspapers spread the rumour that Marcel had
four stomachs, like a cow, which was why he was
able to produce so much of the stuff.

The largest number of sick-bags filled on a
single flight is 390, by the 263 contestants
of the Miss Global Warming Beauty Queen
Competition. Halfway through a bumpy flight
to Bongandanga, they had managed to fill every

sick-bag on the plane. They were then forced to be sick into their posh hats and handbags.

Officers from *The Great Big Book of World Records* went to Bongandanga to measure this extra sick. It filled another 397 sick-bags, making a total of 787.

Enjoy your visit to Spain.

Best wishes
Eric Bibby
Keeper of the Records

PS Why isn't your dad working for his old club, Walchester United? That would be a dream job, wouldn't it?

Danny and Matthew hurried through the Hotel La Langosta on their way to the beach. They noticed Danny's mum and sister Natalie just ahead of them.

'Hey, Nits,' called Danny. 'Fancy a game of football?'

'As if!' replied Natalie, scornfully. 'We're going shopping.'

'Shopping!' complained Danny. 'That's all girls think about. If this new baby Mum's going to have is a girl, I'm coming to live at your house, Matt.'

They stepped from the cool hotel into the oven-like heat outside.

'Hot,' gasped Danny.

'Cool!' said Matthew.

The two boys headed for the beach, where the Kids' Club at the hotel had arranged a game of football.

It was a great match. The sand was hard and

flat, and many of the kids who were playing were pretty good.

Danny stood in his goalmouth, watching a girl who looked about his age playing for the other team. She was quick, and she did step-overs and back-heels. Matthew was struggling to mark her and, once, the girl even nutmegged him. Danny could see Matt wasn't happy.

She had a shot like a cannon. Several times she blasted a fizzer towards Danny's goal, but Danny was always equal to it.

'You're good,' the girl remarked after Danny had just tipped her diving header around the post.

'You're brilliant!' said Danny.

'I play striker for Bunbury Bantams. I scored thirty-one goals last season,' boasted the girl.

'I *saved* eighty-seven goals *in one game* last season!' replied Danny.

Towards the end of the game, the ball was played low and fast towards the girl. Matthew was close behind her. She went to control the ball, but at the last moment, lifted her foot and let it pass by.

Matthew was completely fooled. The ball sped past him on one side, while the girl slid past him on the other. His legs went in two directions, and he stumbled and landed on his back.

She was through, with only Danny to beat!

Danny moved quickly off his line. The girl glanced up, and shaped to blast a shot. Danny stopped and braced himself to dive, but she didn't shoot. Instead, she chipped the ball high over Danny's head.

He was caught off balance, and had to watch it soar through the clear blue sky and loop down into his empty net.

GOAL!

The girl disappeared in a scrum of kids as her team mobbed her.

Danny knelt on the sand and stared at the ball nestling in the far corner of his goal.

*His goal.*

Matthew joined him. 'That's the first time anyone's scored past you for –' He thought for a moment.

'*Months!*' Danny blurted out.

'Fourteen months, three weeks, and . . . five days, to be exact.'

Danny and Matthew gazed across the sand as the girl broke away from the throng of kids, did a back somersault, and landed nimbly on her feet.

'Wow!' admired Matthew. 'I can't do that.'

'Neither can I,' admitted Danny. 'I'd better get practising.'

She trotted over to them. She had the reddest hair and greenest eyes Danny had ever seen.

'Hiya.' She grinned. 'I'm Sally Butterworth. See you later in the pool.'

# The Girl

Later that afternoon, Danny and Matthew stood in the shallow end of the hotel pool, playing keepy-uppy headers with a beach ball. They had got to twenty-one, when Sally Butterworth launched herself from the edge of the pool and caught the ball in mid-air, before splashing into the water between the two friends.

'Hiya,' spluttered Sally when she surfaced. She was wearing a pair of red goggles and a snorkel. 'Watch this.'

Sally ducked her head beneath the water and blew a towering spout from the snorkel high into the air.

'Wow!' said Danny and Matthew together. It was one of the best super volcanoes they'd ever seen.

'How high did it go?' asked Sally.

'About one and a bit metres,' replied Danny.

'My record's three metres. No one's beat it at my school. Bet you can't beat it either.'

'Bet I can!' said Danny.

He grabbed his own snorkel from the side of the pool, took a deep breath, then dipped beneath the water and blew out as hard as he could. He heard the spluttering, farty sound and knew he hadn't done it right.

'I won!' cheered Sally. 'Want a race? I've got the Bunbury Belugas Swimming Club record for the Fastest Length of Butterfly Ever.'

'Do you like trying to break records then?'

asked Danny with a slight tremble in his voice.

'Yeah. I broke the school squinting record last month. Watch this.'

Sally made her eyes roll to the centre, as though she was looking at something on the end of her nose. Then her right eye drifted across to look away from her. It moved back to the centre, and her left eye slid across to look away. Then *it* returned to the middle once more.

'Ace,' breathed Danny.

'Cool,' agreed Matthew.

'How long did you squint for when you broke the record?' asked Danny.

'Nine hours, sixteen minutes and seven seconds,' answered Sally. 'It would have been longer, but my mum made me stop.'

Matthew hit the beach-ball high in the air. 'Fancy playing a game?'

'Let's play piggy in the middle,' replied Sally. She glanced at Matthew. 'You can be piggy.'

Matthew grumpily took up position in the centre of the shallow end while the other two went to each side. Sally threw the ball high over Matthew's head. He stretched, but couldn't catch it. Danny returned it, but again Matthew was too short.

'Come on,' called Sally after several minutes. 'At this rate you'll break the record for being the piggy in the middle.'

'I'm fed up with this game,' replied Matthew. 'I'm going to the deep end to practise my diving.'

# The Prawn

The next morning, Sally Butterworth marched up to Danny and Matthew as they were eating breakfast.

'Hiya, Dan!' she called. 'Hiya, Matt.'

Danny noticed that Sally had a large plaster on her knee.

'How did you do that?' he asked.

'My frisbee got stuck in a tree, so I climbed up to get it. I scraped my knee as I came down. I'm going to have a *massive* scab in a couple of days.'

'Ace,' said Danny.

'Cool . . .' agreed Matthew reluctantly.

Sally leaned over and examined Danny's face.

'Wow! Where did all those freckles come from?' she exclaimed. 'You didn't have those yesterday.'

'I always get zillions of freckles when I've been in the sun.'

'Have you ever counted them? It could be a record,' said Sally.

Danny's mouth fell open in amazement. 'Why didn't *I* think of that?'

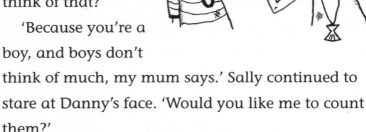

'Because you're a boy, and boys don't think of much, my mum says.' Sally continued to stare at Danny's face. 'Would you like me to count them?'

'Counting's *my* job,' insisted Matthew.

Sally began to count anyway. After a while she said, 'You know, Danny, we could try to break the world record for the Longest Kiss.'

Danny glanced anxiously at Matthew. 'Matt, I think you *had* better do the freckle counting.'

Matthew grabbed Danny and pulled him away. 'We've got to go,' he told Sally.

'See you later, Dan,' she called as the boys raced away.

'Kissing!' said Matthew. 'Gross!'

'Yeah,' agreed Danny. 'Girl-germs! Mega-gross!'

'Lucky I was there to rescue you. *I'll* count your freckles later.'

'Thanks, Matt. I'll have more by tonight anyway.'

Just after lunch, Danny and Matthew arrived at El Estadio del Mar, Real Marisco's home ground, with Danny's mum, dad and sister, Natalie. A large crowd of fans, all wearing the pale pink shirts of Real Marisco, were waiting to greet their possible new manager and his family. They began to cheer loudly, and a flamenco band struck up a jaunty tune, playing with gusto so they could be heard above the din.

The family smiled and waved to the crowd. An odd movement caught Danny's eye. He glanced to his left and was horrified to see a six-foot-tall pink sea creature running towards him. The monster's two long antennae and four of its six outstretched pink legs waggled threateningly.

Before Danny could move or cry out, the creature grabbed him in a fierce, rubbery clinch, and lifted him off the ground. Danny stared into one of its shiny black eyes.

'Matt –' gasped Danny. 'Help!'

Matthew grasped the beast by its feathery, fan-shaped tail.

'Let go of my mate!' he yelled, swinging the creature round.

Cameras flashed. The band played on. The crowd cheered even louder. There was a tearing sound, and without warning, the monster's tail came off in Matthew's hands.

'Arrrrgh!' screamed the sea creature. 'Mi cola!'

It let go of Danny and turned to face Matthew. In the hole where the tail had been, Danny saw a bottom wearing a pair of tight purple underpants.

The tailless monster held two pink claws over its rear end and scuttled away through the crowd.

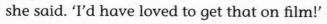

Mum laughed. 'I wish the video camera wasn't broken,' she said. 'I'd have loved to get that on film!'

'Thanks, Matt,' said Danny. 'What was *that*?'

Danny's dad was red-faced with laughter.

'Didn't I tell you?' he replied. 'Real Marisco are known as "Las Gambas", which means "The Prawns" in Spanish. That was their mascot, Gogo La Gamba.'

Matthew gazed at the giant pink tail he still held in his hands.

'Their mascot's a prawn?' he asked disbelievingly.

'That's even worse than Wally the Wall!' exclaimed Danny.

(Wally the Wall was Walchester

United's mascot. He was a brick wall, with legs.)

A man walked towards them, laughing heartily. He shook Dad's hand and then kissed Danny's mum on both cheeks.

Dad turned to the children and introduced the man.

'Kids, this is Señor Pez, the Director of Real Marisco.' He leaned over to the boys and whispered, 'He's the Boss.'

'Delighted to meet you!' said Señor Pez, shaking Danny's hand.

He turned to greet Matthew, who was still clutching the prawn's giant tail.

'I'm sorry,' mumbled Matthew. 'It just came off in my hand.' Señor Pez laughed again. 'Do not be upset, young señor. I hate that stupid prawn.'

He took the tail from Matthew and put it under
his arm. Then he kissed Danny's sister Natalie on
the cheek. She blushed a deeper pink than the giant
prawn.

'Señor Baker, Señora Baker, in two weeks' time,
it is Marisco's annual Festival of Deliverance. In
honour of your visit, the town council of Marisco
would like your son Danny to be "El Periquito".'

'Who's El Periquito?' asked Danny.

'A . . . how do you say it in English? A
butterygar?'

Danny frowned. 'A butterygar?'

Matthew flicked
quickly through his
English-Spanish
dictionary.
'"Periquito"
means
budgerigar,'
he whispered
to Danny.

Señor Pez smiled, and held his hands as though praying. 'The butterygar was sent from heaven to save our town from disaster, many, many years ago,' he explained.

'What do I have to do?'

'Dress up as a bird, climb a tall tree, whistle a special tune and collect caterpillars in a bucket.'

'Ace!' yelled Danny.

'Cool!' agreed Matthew.

# Freckles and
# Jenny-ticks

Hotel La Langosta
Marisco
Spain

Dear Mr Bibby,

It's me again, Danny. The Hotel La Langosta
is Ace. I've met a girl called Sally Butterworth,
who is brilliant at football and likes breaking
records! She's got double-
jointed elbows and she can
climb trees and wiggle her
ears and squint. What's the
world record for squinting?

1,246 freckles

It's really sunny here, and
I've got 1,246 freckles on

my face. It would have been more, but my mum spotted them, and got me with factor 5 million suncream.

Matt counted my freckles using a magic marker pen to mark each one, so he didn't count any twice. The trouble is, the ink won't wash off, so now I've got 1,246 blue dots on my face as well as the freckles.

I think it looks Ace.

Matthew thinks it looks cool.

My sister Natalie thinks it looks stupid.

Sally Butterworth thinks it looks like warpaint.

My mum thinks it looks like a disease.

My dad thinks that if he joins up all the dots, he could make a picture of England's winning goal in the 1966 World Cup Final.

Have I broken the freckles record?

Best wishes
Danny Baker

PS While I'm here in Marisco, I have to dress up
as a budgie called El Periquito, climb
a tall tree, whistle a special tune
and catch caterpillars in a bucket.
I'm not sure why, but I'm going to
have a go! I'll see if I can whistle for
longer and catch more caterpillars than anyone
else has ever done.

El Periquito

The Great Big Book
of World Records
London

ARE YOU A RECORD
BREAKER?

Dear Danny,

Thanks for your letter. Sally Butterworth
sounds an interesting girl.

Your attempt to break the world record for
Freckles on a Single Face was superb, and was
only 453 freckles short. Another day or two
might have given you the extra needed. But
don't be cross with your mum - she was doing
the right thing using suncream on you. Better
safe than sorry!

You asked about the world record for squinting.
That is held by Vinay Adatia, of Mysore, in
India. Unfortunately, Vinay wasn't *trying* to
break the record. When he was ten years old, a
mosquito landed on the end of his nose. Young

Vinay screwed up his face, and squinted to look
at it. At that very moment, the wind changed
direction, and Vinay got stuck like that.

He stayed stuck like that for the next fifteen
years, four months and nineteen days.

Of course, the wind changed again many, many
times during those years, but Vinay's squint
was so well and truly jammed, it wouldn't
budge.

Eventually, Vinay got a job looking after
Radha, the sacred elephant, at the Hindu shrine
near Dooda Bellalu. One morning, he was washing
Radha's hind parts with a scrubbing brush,
when the elephant broke wind so hard and with
such a horrible pong, that not only did it blow
Vinay's hat off, it blew his squint off too! He
is now a famous Bollywood film star.

The record for Non Wind-assisted Squinting is

five days, sixteen hours and thirty-one minutes, held by Franz Überburger, of Wörgl, Austria. His attempt came to an end when he fell asleep from exhaustion, and his eyes returned to their normal position.

If you are going to attempt the squinting record, Danny, be like Franz Überburger, and make sure you try it out of the wind, and away from sacred elephants. Getting stuck with a squint would definitely affect your goalkeeping!

Best wishes
Eric Bibby
Keeper of the Records

Danny and Sally sat on the low wall that enclosed the garden of the Hotel La Langosta. Nearby, Matthew played table tennis with Natalie.

Click-clock, click-clock, click-clock.

Sally stuck her tongue out at Danny. It rolled into a perfect tube.

'Now you try,' she said.

Danny tried, but failed. His tongue just twisted, or bent inwards. 'I can't do it,' he moaned.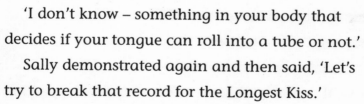

Sally shrugged. 'My mum says it's jenny-ticks.'

'What's jenny-ticks?'

'I don't know – something in your body that decides if your tongue can roll into a tube or not.'

Sally demonstrated again and then said, 'Let's try to break that record for the Longest Kiss.'

'No, I don't think so,' answered Danny.

Click-clock, click-clock, click-clock.

'Why not?' Sally leaned her face closer to Danny's.

Danny gulped.

Her face was so close, it filled his view. Everything had gone silent, and all Danny could hear was his heart bashing inside his chest. Suddenly, Sally's face disappeared, and a ping-pong bat filled his view instead.

'Fancy a game, you two?' asked Matthew.

'What?' Danny blinked, and gazed up at Matthew.

'You and me against Nat the Nit and Sally Butterfingers.' Sally glared at Matthew as he yanked Danny off the chair and dragged him over to the ping-pong table.

Natalie grinned at her brother and sang, 'Danny's kissed his girlfriend, Danny's kissed his girlfriend.'

'I didn't!' protested Danny.

'Well, you would have, if Matt hadn't stepped in.'

Danny blushed prawn-pink.

'No I wouldn't,' he said quietly. 'And she's not my girlfriend. Come on, let's play.'

Click-clock, click-clock, click-clock.

Every time Danny glanced across the table at Sally, she smiled at him.

Matthew smacked Danny on the top of his arm with his ping-pong bat. 'Keep your mind on the game!' he hissed. 'They're winning!'

Danny tried. He tried hard, but it seemed that every time he hit the ball, it either pinged into the net, or ponged on to the floor. Finally he looped a weak shot into the air to make sure it got over the net. Natalie pounced on it, and smashed the ball back at him.

'Yesssssss! The Girls beat the Boys!'

Natalie and Sally high-fived, and did a silly victory dance around the table.

'See you at dinner, losers!' yelled Natalie as she walked away laughing.

Matthew glared at Danny.

'You were useless,' he snarled.

'You . . . you kept getting in my way,' countered Danny.

'*Me?* You couldn't get the ball on the table!'

'Yeah, because –'

Before Danny could finish, Matthew threw his bat down on the table and stormed off.

'Matt!' called Danny, but his friend carried on walking. Danny looked at Sally. She rolled her eyes. 'Urgh! Boys!'

# Silly Sausage

Hotel La Langosta
Marisco
Spain

Dear Mr Bibby

I'm the Marisco Junior Chorizo-pushing
Champion! This morning some of the kids'
Club here at the hotel entered the annual
championships. You have to use your nose to push
a Spanish sausage along the ground for as far
as you can. It was fun!

Matthew dropped out pretty quickly, and so did
all the other kids, except for Sally Butterworth.
My knees and hands and back were killing me,
but I wouldn't give up and neither would
Sally. In the end, Sally had to stop when
the big scab came off her knee, but I

Sally's
knee

**155**

went on for another fifteen laps of the course. I pushed the chorizo sausage for 8.88 km.

Matthew says that Sally let me win, but I think he's just jealous.

I won a gold medal shaped like a sausage. It's not *real* gold, but it's still Ace. The local chorizo-pushing team have asked me if I want to be in their squad when we come out to live here. They've never won the Spanish Chorizo-pushing Cup, and want to get the best players they can. I might do it!

medal

Can you tell me, has anyone ever pushed a chorizo further than 8.88 km? I'm very stiff and sore today, and I've got to do the 'El Periquito' thing in a few days. I hope I've not spoilt my chances to break *that* record.

Best wishes
Danny

ARE YOU A RECORD
BREAKER ?

Dear Danny

Congratulations on winning the Marisco Junior
Chorizo-pushing Championship. I'm sorry, but
your excellent performance was many shoves
short of the world record.

In 2000, to celebrate the birth of the new
millennium, Luis 'La Nariz' Lopo set off from
Madrid in an attempt to push a chorizo sausage
around the world with his nose, in a symbolic
gesture to bring about world peace. He had
pushed the sausage for 3,932.6 km, when his
route took him across Red Square in Moscow,
Russia, during a military parade. Tragically,
because 'La Nariz' was so close to the ground,
he wasn't seen, and was run over by a Russian
T-90S tank.

Amazingly, although the tank squashed most of Luis, it completely missed his nose *and* the chorizo, both of which can now be seen, stuffed and on display, in the museum of his home town, Fisgón.

Good luck with the 'El Periquito' ceremony, Danny.

Best wishes
Eric Bibby
Keeper of the Records

It was early in the morning on the day of
the ceremony. Sally Butterworth
sat close to Danny, trying to
teach him how to waggle
his ears. Danny's face
twitched and convulsed
with the effort.

Sally grabbed
Danny's ears, and
wiggled them.

'You need to move
*this* part of your head –'
she slapped him on the forehead – 'not *that* part of
your head.'

'It's no good,' complained Danny. 'I can't do it.'

Sally smiled.

Oh-oh! thought Danny. She's got that 'Kiss-Me-
Quick' look again!

He felt someone grab his arm and drag him on
to his feet. It was Matthew.

'Come on, it's time you put your budgie costume
on,' said his friend.

Danny yanked his arm free of Matthew's grasp.

'Stop dragging me around, and telling me what to do,' he snapped.

'I'm just looking out for you,' replied Matthew.

'I can look out for myself, *thanks*. You're worse than Mum.'

'Yeah?'

'Yeah.'

'Right, if that's how you feel, you stay here, canoodling with your *girlfriend*.'

Sally giggled.

'I will if I want to,' said Danny. 'You're just jealous.'

'Yeah, right!'

'Yeah, *right*!'

Matthew strode away.

'I hope the caterpillars get you, Budgie-face!' he called over his shoulder.

Danny tried to think of something snotty to say back to Matthew. He couldn't. They had never fallen out before.

'Get lost!' he shouted, but he didn't really mean it.

Sally rolled her eyes again. 'Urgh! Boys!'

# El Periquito

In the hotel bedroom, Danny's mum put down the video camera that she had been trying to mend in time for the ceremony. Then she helped him put on the bird costume.

'You're very quiet,' she said as Danny stepped into his pink, three-toed budgie feet. 'Is everything all right?'

Danny shrugged. 'Yeah.'

Mum began to pull the bright blue stretchy tights up Danny's legs.

'Mum, why am I doing this?' he grumbled.

'I thought you wanted to do it.'

Danny sighed. 'I do, but what's it all about?'

Mum held up the budgie suit. It was covered in vivid sky-blue feathers, with black and white striped wings sown along the arms, and a short, pointed black and white tail.

'There's an ancient tree in the centre of the town square that is supposed to have been planted by Saint Peter of the Fishes, Marisco's patron saint. The locals believe that while the tree is alive their fishermen will continue to catch plenty of seafood . . .'

Danny put his arms into the budgie wings. Mum joined the two parts of the body together, and began to fumble with the zip.

'Over a hundred years ago, the tree was infested with a plague of caterpillars that all hatched out on the same night and began to munch away at the leaves. The townsfolk prayed for a miracle to save their tree, and the miracle arrived the next morning, when a blue and white budgie flew into town and ate all the caterpillars.'

She pulled the zip carefully towards Danny's neck.

'El Periquito – the budgie – saved the tree from certain death and saved the fishermen from going out of business. As it munched away, the bird filled the square with its chirpy song. Then, when it had eaten every caterpillar, the budgie flew away, never to return.'

Mum slid the tight white hood over Danny's head and fitted it snugly around his chin. She smoothed down the four black feathered spots around his neck and fixed the stubby yellow beak over his nose.

'The caterpillars still hatch out on the same day every year, but there's usually only a few hundred or so. A young boy climbs the tree dressed as El Periquito, collects them in a bucket and whistles the "Budgie Song", which I'm told was composed in 1876 by a man named Manuel de Compostela.'

She straightened the suit around Danny's body, and smiled.

'Lovely. Go and look at yourself.'

Danny rustled over to the full-length mirror on the wardrobe door. He lifted his arms to spread his wings, and whistled a few bars of the Budgie Song.

'Ace,' he said.

But he didn't really mean it.

Half an hour later, Danny stood in the town square of Marisco, dressed in the budgie suit and carrying a bucket. The sun had risen above the roofs of the old pink buildings that formed the square, and Danny was already hot.

It seemed like the whole town had come out to see him. The same band that had greeted them at the stadium played the same loud, cheerful tune. Gogo La Gamba, the giant prawn mascot of Real Marisco, had a new tail and was there to cheer Danny on.

Danny's dad stood next to him. He glanced around the crowd.

'Why did Matt decide to stay at the hotel?' he asked.

Danny shrugged. 'Don't know.'

'Have you two fallen out?'

Danny shrugged again, but said nothing. He wished he hadn't told Matthew to 'Get lost!'

Sally Butterworth was standing nearby and blew him a kiss. Danny rolled his eyes.

The Mayoress of Marisco, Señora Juanita Delgardo, held up her hand, and the band and the crowd fell silent.

'Today is the anniversary of our Deliverance from the Plague of Caterpillars,' she announced. 'It is the day the caterpillars hatch out in our sacred tree, and the day El Periquito climbs into the tree to collect them.'

The crowd applauded.

'I now ask Father Ignatius, from the Church of the Holy Budgerigar, to bless El Periquito and send him on his sacred task.'

An old priest stepped forward, placing his hand on Danny's head. The priest mumbled a prayer

in Latin and
sprinkled Danny
with Holy
water. He
crossed
himself,
then
gestured for Danny to climb the tree.

Danny marched forward to the ladders propped
up against the trunk of the massive old tree. A net
stretched around the base of the tree to catch him if
he fell.

'When do I start to whistle?' he asked.

'From the moment you pick up the first
caterpillar to the moment you collect the final one,'
answered Father Ignatius. 'El Periquito sang as he
munched, from start to finish.'

Danny had been learning the Budgie Song for
days. He pursed his lips, and blew. The notes trilled
and echoed around the silent square. When he got
to the top of the ladder and climbed into the tree,
the crowd cheered.

Danny waved. He scanned the crowd quickly, to see if Matthew had turned up to watch him after all, but he couldn't see his friend anywhere. Sally waved back at him.

Danny turned and looked at the branches around him. He gasped.

'What is wrong, Señor Danny? Are there no caterpillars?' called the Mayoress.

'There are *thousands* of them!'

The Mayoress went pale and held on to the priest's arm.

'*Thousands?*'

'Millions!' confirmed Danny. 'They're everywhere!'

He stared goggle-eyed at the green and yellow caterpillars that were crawling over every inch of bark and leaf.

The band fell silent. Hushed, horrified whispers rippled through the townsfolk.

'It has happened again!' said Father Ignatius. 'The plague has returned!'

'Shall we send more people up into the tree?' suggested the Mayoress.

'No!' cried Father Ignatius. 'It must be El Periquito who collects the caterpillars!'

The old priest gazed up at Danny with red, watery eyes.

'Only Danny Baker can save us now!'

# The Kissing Tree

Danny toiled all day in the scorching sun, working his way higher and higher into the tree, picking the small wriggling creatures from underneath leaves, knocking them off twigs and dropping them into buckets. All the time he worked, Danny whistled the Budgie Song.

His limbs ached, his lips ached, but he carried on collecting and he carried on whistling, only stopping to drink water.

The sun dropped lower in the sky. The light began to fade. The mood of the people gathered around the tree was sombre and tense. They all

stood gazing up anxiously at Danny as he crawled
to the tip of the final branch.

He dropped the last caterpillar into
his bucket.

'Finished!' he called hoarsely, and
carried on whistling.

The roar from the throng of people
watching Danny echoed around the
square. It was as though Real Marisco had
won the Cup!

Father Ignatius put his hands together and
offered a silent prayer of thanks.

Danny began to pick his way slowly and
painfully back down through the branches, but
then stopped. His limbs and lips, tight and tense
all day from climbing, gripping and whistling, had
finally given up. Danny's body and mouth locked
tight with cramp.

He couldn't move a muscle.

He couldn't say a word.

He was stuck.

He heard someone below shout, 'Help him!'

Then he heard Sally Butterworth yell, 'I'll save you, Danny!'

Sally raced from the crowd and scurried up the ladder. In seconds she had clambered into the tree and reached the branch where Danny was perched. She smiled at him.

'Your lips are stuck in *kissing* position,' she said.

No! thought Danny. Help!

But there was no one to help. Sally leaned forward and planted her lips firmly on Danny's.

'Awwwwww,' cooed the crowd.

Urrrrrrgh! thought Danny.

He looked past Sally into the crowded square and spotted his sister Natalie laughing at him. Even worse, his mum had finally fixed the video camera and was *filming* the kiss.

He could hear Natalie singing,
'Danny and Sally, sitting in a tree,
K-I-S-S-I-N-G.'

The kiss went on . . .

**Urrrrrrrrrgh!**

and on . . .

**Urrrrrrrrrrrgh!**

and on . . .

# Urrrrrrrrrrrrrgh!

and on . . .

# Urrrrrrrrrrrrrrgh!

Danny sent up his own silent prayer. *Help!*

And his prayer was answered.

He heard leaves rustling and a branch creaking, and there was Matthew, beside them in the tree.

'Now that's enough of *that*!' ordered Matthew. He tried to drag Sally away, but she clung on tight.

'Sally,' he shouted. 'There's a *massive* spider on your back!'

Danny saw Sally's eyes widen in horror. She pulled away quickly.

'Arrrrrrrrrgh!' she screamed. 'Get it off! Get it off!'

Matthew pretended to brush something off her.

He blew out his cheeks and shook his head. 'Wow,

that was *huge*,' he gasped. He wiggled his fingers. 'It had *really* hairy legs! There must be loads more of them around here.'

Sally screamed. In seconds she was out of the tree and standing in the square next to her mother.

Matthew grinned. 'I think Silly Butterworm has just broken the world record for the Fastest Climbing Out of a Tree to Escape an Invisible Spider, don't you?'

Danny looked at Matthew and raised his eyebrows, which was the only part of him he could move. Thanks, Matt, he thought. You saved me.

'I'm sorry, Dan,' said Matthew.

Danny twitched his eyebrows once. So am I, Matt, he thought.

Matthew understood and nodded. 'We will never, *ever* fall out, *ever* again.'

Danny raised his eyebrows twice: No.

'Do you see what happens when I'm not around to look out for you?'

Danny twitched his eyebrows once: Yeah.

The two boys perched side by side in the tree, and

looked down on the people celebrating in the town square. After a while, Matthew sighed.

'Have you realized that when your dad gets the job as manager of Real Marisco, you'll have to live here and I'll have to go back to England?' he said.

Danny frowned: What?

Matthew stared at Danny sadly.

'We'll probably never see each other again,' he said quietly. 'Ever.'

Danny's eyebrows nearly twitched off his face: Nooooooooooooooo!

# Danny Baker - Record Breaker

Hotel La Langosta
Marisco
Spain

Dear Mr Bibby,

I dressed up as El Periquito and collected 14,975 caterpillars. I didn't know it at the time, but as I passed the buckets down to Father Ignatius, Matthew was counting the caterpillars in each one, so that I could write to you with my score. I also stayed in the tree whistling for ten hours and twenty-three minutes. When I'd finished, I had cramp in my whole body. I couldn't move for fifty-three

hours and sixteen minutes. Surely one of these
must be a record?

Best wishes
Danny

The Great Big Book
of World Records
London

ARE YOU A RECORD
BREAKER?

Dear Danny

Fantastic! You saved Marisco from disaster,
and claimed not just one, but *two* El
Periquito world records. You beat the previous
caterpillar-collecting record by more than
thirteen thousand, and whistled in the tree
for nearly ten hours longer than anyone had
ever done before. I'm sure your records will
remain for a very long time, possibly for ever.
Congratulations!

Unfortunately, however, the long attack of
cramp you suffered is not a record.

In 1966, Harriet Snood of Tolpuddle attempted to
break the world record for dancing 'The Twist'.
After sixty-nine hours and seventeen minutes,

her whole body locked like stone.
Doctors have been unable to thaw out
Harriet's frozen muscles even
to this day. She is still stuck
in twisting position! With
every minute that passes, she
adds to her record, which as I
write is 15,696 days, 3 hours
and 6 minutes. Harriet now has
a successful career as a 'Living Sculpture'.

Finally, Danny, you didn't tell me about the
kiss!

Your mum sent me the video she made of you
and Sally Butterworth kissing in the tree. I'm
delighted to tell you that you and Sally have
set a new world record, and I have included
two extra certificates, one for you and one for
Sally. Would you please pass it on to her?

Congratulations on breaking three world

records at once, Danny!

Best wishes
Eric Bibby
Keeper of the Records

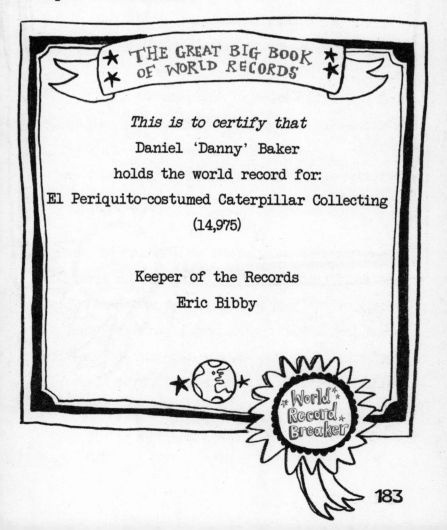

THE GREAT BIG BOOK OF WORLD RECORDS

*This is to certify that*
Daniel 'Danny' Baker
holds the world record for:
El Periquito-costumed Caterpillar Collecting
(14,975)

Keeper of the Records
Eric Bibby

World Record Breaker

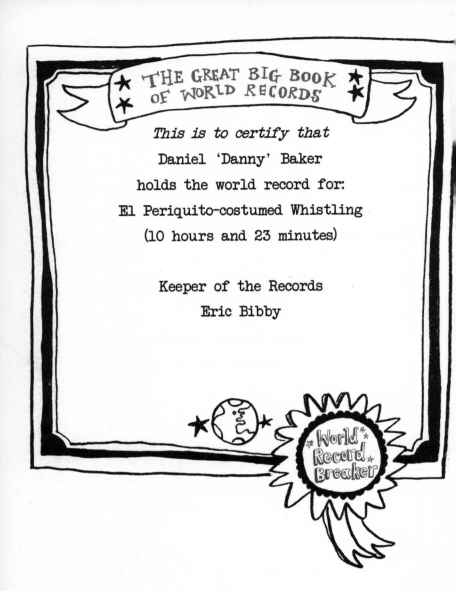

THE GREAT BIG BOOK OF WORLD RECORDS

*This is to certify that*
Daniel 'Danny' Baker
holds the world record for:
El Periquito-costumed Whistling
(10 hours and 23 minutes)

Keeper of the Records
Eric Bibby

World Record Breaker

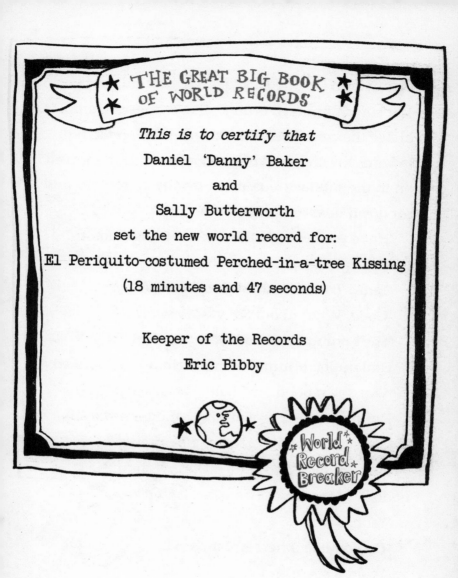

THE GREAT BIG BOOK
OF WORLD RECORDS

*This is to certify that*
Daniel 'Danny' Baker
and
Sally Butterworth
set the new world record for:
El Periquito-costumed Perched-in-a-tree Kissing
(18 minutes and 47 seconds)

Keeper of the Records
Eric Bibby

World Record Breaker

Danny and his dad kicked a ball around the beach. The sun shimmered orange, like a huge satsuma, above the calm blue sea. Danny dribbled the ball towards his dad, and nutmegged him. Dad toppled on to the sand with a groan. Danny came over and sat down next to him.

'Have you and Matthew made friends again?' asked Dad.

'Yeah, 'course we have,' replied Danny.

'Good. What about Sally Butterworth?'

'She's going home today.'

Dad nudged Danny with his elbow and winked.

'Was she a good girlfriend?' he asked.

Danny blushed prawn-pink, and looked away.

'She was a good *footballer*,' he answered.

Dad laughed and ruffled Danny's hair. He nodded at the view. 'Fantastic, isn't it?'

'Yeah.'

'Do you like it here in Marisco?'

'Yeah, it's Ace.'

'Would you like to live here for good?'

Danny pushed his feet into the sand and hugged

his knees. 'Could Matt come and live here too?'

'No, of course not. His mum and dad couldn't just pack up and move out here because we have.'

Dad put his arm around Danny's shoulders.

'Honestly, where would you rather live, here or in England?'

Danny took a deep breath. 'In England!' he blurted out. 'I'm sorry, Dad. I'd be OK living here, honest, but I'd have to spend every day wearing factor 5 million suncream, and I'd miss the rain at home, and I'd miss my school football team, and . . . I'd miss Matt. He's my best mate.'

Dad frowned and looked thoughtful. 'Yeah, I thought you'd say that.' A grin spread slowly across his face. 'Good thing I turned down the Manager's job here at Real Marisco then.'

'What?'

'Walchester United want me to be their goalkeeping coach. It's my Dream Job, Danny. I start as soon as we get back.'

Danny jumped up. 'Are you serious?'

'Totally.'

Danny punched the air, put his head back and yelled, 'IN . . . THE . . . NET!'

When they got back to the hotel, Sally Butterworth was waiting in reception for the bus to go back to the airport. Matthew was there too, to make sure she didn't miss it.

'Bye, Danny,' said Sally as the bus pulled up.

'Er . . . bye, Sally.' Danny stood well back, in case she had any goodbye kissing in mind.

'Did you know, Father Ignatius, of the Church of the Holy Budgerigar, has said that from now on "El Periquito" must be kissed by a beautiful young girl before he comes down from the tree? Why don't we come back next year and try to break our own record?'

Danny and Matthew looked at each other.

'*Not* Ace!' cried Danny.

'*Not* cool!' agreed Matthew.

Sally got on board the bus and waved sadly through the back window as it pulled away.

Danny's mum walked up to them.

'Have you two boys packed yet?' she asked. 'We'll be leaving after lunch.'

Danny grinned at Matthew. 'Come on, Matt – cola and paella for lunch,' he said. 'I've got sick-bags to fill!'

# The
# Super-Secret
# Ingredient

WARNING!
LOW-FLYING
COWPATS
AHEAD

# The Pongy Potion

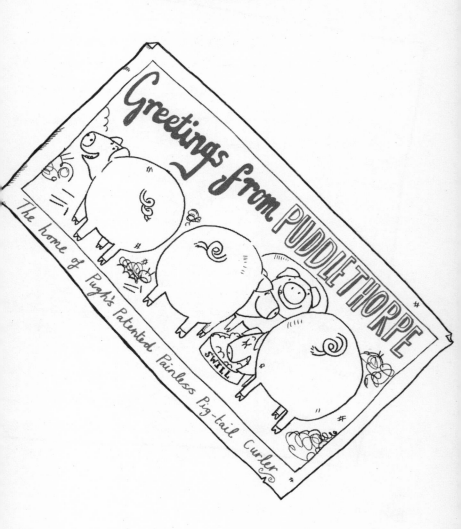

Crag Top Farm, Puddlethorpe

Dear Mr Bibby

I'm staying on Grandma Florrie and Grandad Nobby's farm. It's slippy and slimy and whiffs for England! My best friend Matthew's here too. We're having fun tidying up cowpats, making mudslides, eating beans, feeding the pigs with something called Swill, and brewing up a Pongy Potion in a bucket! This morning I stacked five dried cowpats on my head and walked 6.7 km. I would have gone further, but it started to rain and the cowpats turned to mush and dribbled down all over me. My grandma says 'A bit of muck never hurt anyone.' I don't think my mum would say that. Did I break a record?

Best wishes
Danny Baker

cowpat

mushy cowpat

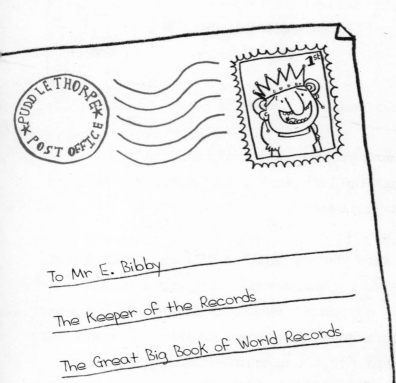

To Mr E. Bibby

The Keeper of the Records

The Great Big Book of World Records

London

ARE YOU A RECORD
BREAKER ?

Dear Danny

Thank you for your postcard. I had no idea
that the Painless Pig-tail Curler was invented
in Puddlethorpe.

I *know* you and Matthew will have lots of fun
on your grandparents' farm, but I wouldn't
try any cowpat records if I were you. There are
Professional Cowpatters all over the world who
compete in tournaments, either individually
or in teams, battling to be the best at cowpat
balancing, cowpat rolling, cowpat tossing,
cowpat spinning and cowpat polo. Tournament-
standard cowpats are produced from carefully
bred Culworth Curly-horn cows, which are fed
a special diet to give the pats a regular
consistency. They are baked in clay ovens for

one hour and thirteen minutes exactly, at a
temperature of 190° centigrade (Gas Mark 5), and
then cut to the regulation 35 cm-diameter size.
All record attempts are strictly controlled
by the WPCA (World Professional Cowpatting
Association).

However, don't let that stop you having fun
with cowpats!

Best wishes
Eric Bibby
Keeper of the Records

PS Is your grandad the same Norbert 'Nobby'
Baker who broke the world record for Blindfold
One-foot Keepy-uppies in 1968?

Danny and Matthew sat at the big kitchen table, eating lunch. On the plates in front of them, Grandma Florrie's home-made baked beans dripped and dribbled over the toast. Grandma was proud of her beans, and gave them to the boys at every meal whether they wanted them or not. 'They'll put hairs on your chest,' she told them. Every night, they stood in front of the bathroom mirror and checked, but so far nothing had happened.

Grandma sat in a battered old armchair in her bright floral apron and green wellington boots, and got on with her knitting. She was making pink bootees for Mum's new baby.

Danny frowned. 'How do you know the baby's going to be a girl?' he asked.

'I can feel it in my waters,' she replied mysteriously.

Grandad Nobby sat at the table with the boys, reading Mr Bibby's letter. The grubby old flat cap that he always wore was pushed back on his head. Danny couldn't remember seeing Grandad without his cap – he suspected he even slept in it.

'Aye, Danny, that's me,' confirmed Grandad Nobby. 'You're not the only one in the family who likes to break records, you know.'

'It must be jenny-ticks,' commented Matthew.

Grandad walked over to a cupboard and rummaged around inside.

Danny and Matthew took their chance while Grandma and Grandad weren't looking, and quickly scraped most of their beans into a bowl they had hidden under the table.

'Ah, here it is,' muttered Grandad after a few seconds, and handed Danny a picture frame.

Beneath the glass, he saw a familiar-looking certificate.

★ THE GREAT BIG BOOK ★
OF WORLD RECORDS

*This is to certify that*
Norbert 'Nobby' Baker
holds the world record for:
Blindfold One-foot Keepy-uppies
(163)


Keeper of the Records
Alfred Bibby

★ World ★
Record
★ Breaker ★

'Ace!' said Danny.

'Cool,' agreed Matthew. 'But if you were so good at football, Mr B, why did you give it up and become a farmer?'

'Tell Matt your story, Grandad,' urged Danny. 'Tell him about the Rotting Chowhabunga.'

Grandad's brow furrowed as though he was remembering something painful. 'I didn't *want* to give up football, Matt,' he said. 'I was *forced* to give it up.'

'Why?'

'Injury,' he replied, and held his left knee.

'Was it a bad tackle?' guessed Matthew. 'Did another player go over the top of the ball? Did you land badly going for a header?'

Grandad Nobby was silent for a moment. He shook his head slowly.

'I trod on a seed-pod,' he said eventually.

Matthew stared at him blankly.

'I was on a tour of Brazil with Walchester United. I'd heard that the Rotting Chowhabunga plant was about to flower in the jungle. It's supposed to have the Stinkiest Flower in the world, and local people say that anyone who gets too close to its horrible stench is instantly turned to stone!'

Matthew's jaw dropped. 'Is that true?'

'Of course not!' chuckled Grandad. 'It's just a myth! People can't be petrified by a pong!' He ruffled Matthew's hair. 'Anyway, the Rotting Chowhabunga

only blooms in the wild and the petals last for just one day, so I hurried out into the jungle to see it. But when I got to the spot, I was too late: the flower had died. As I turned away, I slipped on a seed-pod that had fallen on the ground, and twisted my knee so badly I never played football again.'

He rubbed his leg once more.

'A seed from the pod got stuck in my sock. I found it when I got home a week later, so I planted the seed in some soil and it grew. Ever since, I've been determined to be the first person to get the Rotting Chowhabunga to bloom in a pot. That plant ended my football career, and I'm not going to let it beat me again!'

Matthew glanced nervously around the room. 'Where is it?'

'It's in a pot, out near the vegetable patch,' answered Grandma. 'If your Grandad ever wins the battle, and it's even *half* as stinky as he says it'll be, then I don't want that thing anywhere near my house.'

'How long have you been trying to make it

flower?' asked Matthew.

'Thirty-nine years,' replied Grandad. 'I use
soil from my compost heap, and feed it with the
gunge from my barrel of liquid cowpats. The plant
grows beautifully, but I can't find that one special
ingredient that will make it flower.' He
shook his head thoughtfully. 'I will
one day though, you see if I don't.'

Suddenly, Danny had an idea.
He glanced over at Matthew and
winked.

Grandad sighed. 'I don't
have much luck with my veggies
either. It's the Puddlethorpe Annual
Country Fair in a few days, and I never win first
prize. Every year, Ernie Slack manages to beat me
into second place. I don't know how he does it.'

After lunch, Danny and Matthew carried a bucket
of swill across the farmyard to feed Fish, Chips and
Peas, Grandma's three little pigs. Then they went to
check on the Pongy Potion, which was brewing in a
big metal bucket behind the pigsty. Its contents were

cooking slowly in the sun, and for days the boys had been adding all sorts of ingredients to it.

'I've been thinking,' said Danny. 'Do you reckon our Pongy Potion could be the special ingredient Grandad needs to make his Rotting Chowhabunga flower? Let's add it to the gunge in his cowpat barrel and see what happens.'

'I don't *want* it to flower, if it'll turn us into stone,' remarked Matthew.

'Don't be daft, Matt! You heard Grandad – it's just a myth!'

Matthew frowned, but said nothing more.

'Urgh!' cried Danny, covering his face with his arm as they approached the bucket. 'It's getting *really* pongy!'

He held his nose, took off the lid, and the boys peeked inside. It looked like a giant had been sick in the bucket. It was filled almost to the brim with a thick, lumpy greeny-yellowy soup. Wisps of green steam drifted slowly upwards from the surface.

Matthew reached into the pocket of his jeans, and unfolded a piece of paper:

# Pongy Potion Recipe

3 milk bottlefuls of muddy puddle water

99 tea bags (used and soggy)

1 dollop of mud

5 squirts of washing-up liquid

A splodge of cold mashed potato

3 apple cores (Granny Smith's)

A brushful of grey hair (Granny Baker's)

77 carrot tops

1 pineapple yogurt with bits in

A sprinkle of crunched-up eggshells

2 banana skins (squished)

4 rotten tomatoes (squashed)

2 balls of donkey doo-doo

3 handfuls of mouldy straw

A sweaty sock with a hole in the big toe

Half a can of lemonade with the fizz all
   gone

4 finger-scoops of earwax

A munched-up Garibaldi biscuit

A teaspoonful of toenail clippings (assorted)

'I don't remember putting that mushroom in there,' said Danny, tipping in the beans they had saved from lunch.

'We didn't. That's grown since yesterday,' replied Matthew. He wrote '1 mushroom' and '1 bowl of Grandma's home-made baked beans' at the bottom of his list.

The Pongy Potion hissed angrily and a small bubble of gas popped on to the surface. Danny plunged a rusty old trowel into the concoction, and turned it over a few times. The Pongy Potion

gurgled and more bubbles burst from the brew. The smell smashed into Danny's face, drilled up his nostrils and exploded through his brain. He reeled backwards, coughing and gasping for breath.

'Quick!' he spluttered. 'Put the lid back on, before it gets out!'

Matthew slammed the lid on to the bucket and they scuttled away to safety.

'Mega-ace!' cried Danny.

'Mega-cool!' agreed Matthew.

# A Wiggle of Worms

Crag Top Farm
Puddlethorpe

Dear Mr Bibby

Today I sat in a bath full of
worms for four hours and fifty-
five minutes. We dug through
Grandad's gigantic steaming compost
heap and pulled out every worm we could find. It
took us all morning. Matt lost count after 9,183.

worms

I didn't mind the worms wriggling around in my
ears, but I had to stop when some
of them started to crawl up my
nose. In fact, they were getting
everywhere. It definitely wasn't Ace.

Worm
up
nose

Then we had to sneak all the worms out of the bath and back to the compost heap before Grandma realized what we were up to.

Is my four hours and fifty-five minutes in the worm bath a record?

Best wishes
Danny Baker


PS Grandad Nobby *is* the same person who broke the Blindfold One-foot Keepy-uppies Record. I've seen his certificate. It was signed by Alfred Bibby – is that your dad?
PPS While I sat in the bath of worms, Matthew tried to do Blindfold Keepy-uppies. He's only got up to three so far. It's really hard!

The Great Big Book
of World Records
London

ARE YOU A RECORD
BREAKER?

Dear Danny

Thanks for letting me know about your brave
attempt on the Worm-bath Endurance record. You
were exactly seventy-three hours short. The
record is held by Wolfgang Walnuss of Germany.
He owned a worm farm in the town of Worms, and
gave every single worm a name. His favourite
was called Heidi.

Simply sitting in a bath of worms wasn't
enough for Wolfgang. He had a lifelong
ambition to *swim* in worms in Worms.

On the 15 June 1993, Wolfgang filled a swimming
pool with worms and plunged in, but after only
half a length, he sank to the bottom of the worm
pool. Everyone watching searched desperately in

the wriggling, writhing mass, but sadly Wolfgang
Walnuss drowned in worms in Worms.

However, he *did* set a new Worm-swimming world
record of 11.5 m, and his certificate is now
on display in the Worms Town Museum. No one
has ever tried to beat it. As Wolfgang's life
and death show, one worm may be wonderfully
wiggly, but dozens can be dangerously deadly.

Best wishes
Eric Bibby
Keeper of the Records

PS Alfred Bibby *was* my father. He became
fascinated with record-breaking quite by
chance one morning in 1951, when he discovered
the world's biggest ever earwig (34.4 cm long)
hiding in his left wellington boot. I have a
photo of him somewhere holding up the whopper!
If I can find it, I'll send you a copy.

That afternoon, the boys hurried across the farmyard with another bowl of Grandma's baked beans to add to the Pongy Potion.

'Don't you think we've put enough of those beans in?' asked Matthew.

'You can never have too many beans, Matt,' replied Danny. 'And if we don't put them in the potion, we'll have to *eat* them.'

Just then they heard a clanking sound coming from behind the pigsty. When they looked, the lid of the bucket was jumping up and down, as though something inside was trying to get out. Two long, greeny-yellow tentacles crept down the side of the bucket.

'The Pong's alive!' yelled Danny.

With a bang, the lid shot a metre into the air and clattered on to the ground at the boys' feet.

'It's escaping!' cried Matthew.

Danny held his nose, raced to the bucket, and threw in the beans. 'Come on, Matt, it's time to chuck the Pong Monster into Grandad's cowpat barrel before it gets away.'

They grabbed the bucket, and raced across the garden to the vegetable patch. The big wooden barrel stood just inside the gate.

Matthew shoved the lid to one side, and Danny tipped the steaming, bubbling, seething mixture into the thick, browny-black slop. The Pongy Potion floated on the surface for a moment before the cowpat sludge sucked it down hungrily.

LIQUID COWPATS

Suddenly, huge bubbles began to appear, bursting with loud, sloppy pops. The barrel started to grumble loudly.

'That sounds like Dad's stomach after he's had a chicken vindaloo,' laughed Danny.

Something knocked on the inside of the wooden tub. Long ropes of sticky slime spat into the air. The grumbling turned to rumbling and the top of the liquid started to bulge upwards.

'It's going to blow!' yelled Danny. 'It *is* like Dad's stomach after a chicken vindaloo! Run!'

The two boys charged towards the farmhouse as the cowpat barrel erupted with a ground-shaking 'BOOOOOMMM!'.

Danny glanced over his shoulder and saw a plume of browny-greeny-yellowy-black goo rocket into the air. As it climbed higher, it spread out like a fan, casting its smelly contents far and wide, and blotting out the sun.

The shadow of the approaching muck-cloud fell over Danny and Matthew. They nearly made it to the kitchen door, but not quite. They were just a few metres short when the Pong landed.

SPLAT!

The whole garden turned browny-greeny-yellowy-black.

Both boys had been turned into gooey gobs of greasy gloop.

'Ace!' said Danny, pulling a slimy old tea bag off

his head.

'Cool!'

agreed

Matthew.

Grandma

opened the

kitchen door.

'Oh, my days!' she cried. 'What's happened?'

'Grandad's cowpat barrel blew up!' answered
Danny.

'And we *stink*,' grinned Matthew.

'Not for long,' replied Grandma. 'Don't move!'

She marched off around the side of the house,
returning with the hosepipe.

'Keep still,' she ordered, and blasted the yucky
slime off the boys.

Grandad Nobby appeared at the door. 'How did
that get up there?' he asked, pointing to the sock
that dangled drippily from the TV aerial on the
roof.

Danny and Matthew glanced at each other.

'Cats?' suggested Danny.

'Bats?' suggested Matthew.

Grandad took off his old flat cap and scratched his head. He looked around at the mess that covered everything in sight. 'We'll have to hope it rains,' he said.

'Well then, we'd better do the Puddlethorpe Rain Dance,' said Grandma, and she and Grandad set off round the garden, jigging and wailing tunelessly. Danny and Matthew joined in, splashing in the shallow pools of dark sludge.

That evening it rained torrents. 'Never fails,' smiled Grandad, winking at the boys. 'This rain'll wash all that goo down into the ground. It'll be good for the soil, so no harm done.'

'There's harm done to my nose,' complained Grandma. 'What a whiff!'

# Big

Danny woke early the next morning, got out of bed and opened the bedroom curtains.

He gasped.

He rubbed his eyes and looked again.

He gasped for a second time.

'Grandad! Grandma! Matt! Get up! Come and look at this!'

Danny raced downstairs and into the kitchen. He flung open the kitchen door and stared outside. He couldn't help it: he gasped once more.

The grass in the garden was two metres high. Buttercups, daisies and dandelions, with flowers as big as dinner-plates, stretched up above the tall green blades. Rose-bushes stood like small trees down one side of the garden, their branches bending under the weight of enormous white blooms. Other gigantic plants crushed and crowded together nearby, with towering spikes of red and blue flowers, huge purple bells and rafts of pink blossom.

Grandad, Grandma and Matthew joined Danny at the door.

'Oh, my giddy aunt!' exclaimed Grandma. 'I'm going to need a vase as big as a milk churn for those roses.'

'What about your vegetables, Mr B?' asked Matthew.

'My marrows!' yelled Grandad. 'Come on, let's go and see.'

They all pulled on their wellington boots and set off like jungle explorers, pushing aside the tall leaves, treading cautiously through the high grass that rustled noisily in the breeze.

Danny glimpsed woodlice as large as saucers, and spiders bigger than Grandad's hand, scurrying away into the shade.

All around them, but out of sight, hundreds of huge insects hummed and buzzed and clicked. Grandma moved an enormous buttercup leaf to one side, revealing a frog the size of a football staring back at them.

Danny laughed. 'Look at those big bulgy eyes – it looks like our teacher, Mrs Woodcock!'

'Yeah,' agreed Matthew. 'And she's got frog's legs too!'

As they emerged from the grass and gazed over the wall of the vegetable patch, Grandad jumped in the air like he'd scored a goal.

'My Rotting Chowhabunga!' he cried, pointing at his treasured plant.

It was normally a small spiky clump of bright green waxy leaves. Now it was almost as tall as the boys, and rising from the centre was a thick stalk with a large dark flower-bud on the end.

Rotting Chowhisunya

'It's going to flower!' said Grandad.
'For the first time *ever* in a pot! It's a
miracle!'

Danny grinned at Matthew and
winked.

'And my marrows are massive!'
exclaimed Grandad. 'My carrots are
colossal! My lettuces are leviathans! My
gooseberries are gargantuan! My parsnips
are . . .' He thought for a moment '. . . pretty big!'

Grandad's grin got wider.

'If Ernie Slack can beat
these beauties, I'll eat
my cap!' He rubbed
his hands together.
'We'll pick the
best tomorrow
morning and
enter them for
the competition
at the Fair. *This*
year, victory will be mine!'

# A Spot of Bother in the Vegetable Patch

The Great Big Book
of World Records
London

THE GREAT BIG BOOK OF WORLD RECORDS

ARE YOU A RECORD BREAKER?

Dear Danny

Here's the photo I promised you of the humongous earwig! This creature inspired my father to track down and measure the biggest bugs from all over the world, and he donated many of his specimens to Creepy-Crawly Creek, a Wildlife Park and Home for Rescued Invertebrates at Bugsby Tyke. It's actually

WORLD'S BIGGEST EARWIG

Dad, 1951

not far from Puddlethorpe, and I think *you* would love it, because it's a record-breaking kind of place!

They have ants as thick as your thumb, centipedes as long as your leg and slugs as fat as your fist. They have a Spider City, a Beetle Boulevard and a Cockroach Corner. They also have Gastropod Grove, which contains the largest collection of slugs and snails in the world, all slithering and sliming around in a massive compound. This is officially the Slimiest Place in the World, and *has* to be worth a visit!

Best wishes
Eric Bibby
Keeper of the Records

PS The little boy with knobbly knees standing next to my father is me! Believe it or not, I do not have the Knobbliest Knees in the world. That record is held by Alfie Smee, of Beaumont-cum-Moze, whose horrible, ugly knees could make grown women faint and small children cry. They were *so* bad that on 13 May 1932 a Special Law was passed banning Alfie Smee's knees from ever being shown in public.

It was the morning of the Puddlethorpe
Annual Country Fair. Danny and
Matthew sat at the kitchen
table, flicking through a
book called *What's That
Bug?*. Nine enormous pickle
jars, their lids punched
with air holes, were lined up
in front of them, each one
containing a huge crawling insect.

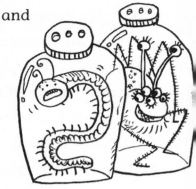

Grandma studied the specimens with interest.

'My,' she said, 'you two *have* been busy. What are
you going to do with these beasties?'

'We're trying to find out what they're called,'
answered Danny. 'Matt's going to measure them
all and I'm going to write to Mr Bibby at *The Great
Big Book of World Records* to see if any of them are
world-beaters.'

Matthew grinned at Danny. 'Imagine if your
sister Natalie found a couple of these under her
duvet . . . !'

Grandad put his head round the kitchen door.

'Hurry up, you two,' he said. 'I'm going to need some help with my vegetables. The sooner they're picked, the sooner we can get to the Fair.'

'OK, Grandad. We'll finish doing this later.' The boys pulled on their wellies and went outside.

The flower-bud on the Rotting Chowhabunga was bigger and darker.

'I think today's the day,' said Grandad excitedly.

'Will the flower *really* stink?' asked Matthew, eyeing the plant warily.

'So I've been told, but I don't know for sure. I've never smelt one.'

Grandad led the way along the narrow path they had cleared through the jungle the day before, towards the gate. The grass, buttercups and dandelions waved high above them in the breeze. As he stepped out, the boys heard him cry out in dismay.

'Oh no! My prize-winners!'

Danny and Matthew ran to his side and looked over the wall. What they saw made their jaws drop.

The vegetable patch was a seething, writhing

mass of gigantic pink worms each at least four
metres long and as thick as a goalpost.

They looked more like pythons
than worms, as they crawled,
slithered and slid over the
huge plants, sucking and
slurping great holes out of
them.

'Gross!' said Danny.

'Double-gross!' added Matthew.

'Quick!' shouted Grandad, grabbing a
wheelbarrow. 'We've got to get the good vegetables
out before those beasts eat them all!'

He trundled his barrow through the gate towards
the one remaining untouched marrow. The boys
helped him lift it into the barrow, then Danny raced
towards the runner beans, while Matthew grabbed
a spade and headed for the onions.

'Only pick the good ones!' called Grandad,
thwacking a monster worm with his flat cap.

Danny had collected an armful of enormous
runner beans when he felt the earth shudder and

shift under his feet. The head of a giant earthworm burst out of the soil, stretching and quivering towards the beans.

Three worms emerged from the ground nearby and headed for the sprouts. Two more appeared by the peas, while others popped up at various places around the patch and began to creep towards the middle, all heading for Grandad's marrow.

Grandma Florrie ran up to the gate.

'Lawks-a-lordy!' she howled. 'What are we going to do?'

'Call Creepy-crawly Creek in Bugsby Tyke!'

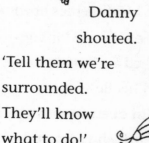

Danny shouted. 'Tell them we're surrounded. They'll know what to do!'

# The Worm Wranglers of Creepy-crawly Creek

Danny scanned the vegetable patch. In a far corner by the gate he spied a large stack of sun-dried cowpats that were piled up ready to be taken to the Fair for the cowpat-hurling contest.

'Come on, Matt, let's get 'em!'

Danny and Matthew began to skim the hard, flat pooh-projectiles at the wiggling monster worms as they burst from their burrows and lunged at the vegetables. Grandad stood guard by his precious marrow, fending off incoming attackers with his spade and cap.

Despite their efforts, the huge worms kept coming. Just when the boys' cowpat ammunition supply was starting to run low, a bright red truck skidded to a halt on the other side of the wall, six yellow lights on top of the cab flashing urgently. Emblazoned along the side of the vehicle were the words:

# CREEPY-CRAWLY
## CREEK
### EMERGENCY WORM-WRANGLING TEAM
'We're Bugsby Tyke's finest!'
(NO JOB TOO LARGE OR TOO WRIGGLY)

A woman and two men jumped down from the truck. They wore lime-green, wipe-clean, slime-proof zip-tight boiler suits, and carried large yellow buckets in their red-rubber-gloved hands.

Hammers, pincers and lassos dangled from their shiny black belts.

'I'm Babs, Chief Worm Wrangler,' announced the woman as she rushed through the gate. 'And this is my team, Bernie and Butch.'

She saw the giant worms slithering all over the vegetable patch. 'Whoa! This is *serious*!'

'We're going to need bigger buckets!' yelled Bernie.

'We're going to need wheelie bins!' barked Butch.

Babs surveyed the scene. 'Right! Here's the plan!' She pointed at Danny and Matthew. 'You lads keep pelting these monsters with cowpats.'

She pointed at Grandma. 'Mrs Baker, take Butch to the wheelie bins.'

She turned to the third Worm Wrangler.

'Bernie, call Base Control. Tell them to get High Containment Unit X1-2000 ready. These are Super Worms we're dealing with!'

When Butch returned with the wheelie bins, Babs slapped Danny and Matthew on the back. 'Well done, lads,' she said. 'You've done a great job. Now it's time to let the professionals take over.'

Babs and Bernie unhooked their lassos and took up position by the marrow in the barrow, snagging each mammoth worm that appeared above ground. As the ropes tightened, the struggling creatures were dragged out of their burrows, and flung wriggling and writhing into the bins. Butch slammed the lids shut as the worms battered against them, trying to escape.

At last the vegetable patch was clear. Babs turned to Grandad. 'The situation's under control now, Mr Baker. You can pick your vegetables and get off to the Fair.'

She strode over to the boys. 'Thanks for all your help, lads. I've never seen worms this big in Yorkshire! The wheelie bins won't hold them for long – we need to get them into the High Containment Unit X1-2000 asap.'

Babs reached into a pocket of her lime-green, wipe-clean, slime-proof zip-tight boiler suit. 'Here's four free tickets for Creepy-crawly Creek,' she said, handing them to Danny. 'You can come and see your worms any time.'

She jumped into the truck next to Bernie and Butch, winked at the boys and, with lights flashing, sped off towards Bugsby Tyke.

'Come on!' said Grandad, grabbing his vegetables. 'Let's get going. I can't wait to see Ernie Slack's face when he catches sight of this little lot!'

# Ernie Slack

As usual, Grandad's neighbour Tom Abson
had made room in his Low Meadow for the
Puddlethorpe Annual County Fair. The field was
a hotch potch of animal pens, stalls and sideshow
attractions, and at its centre stood the candy-striped
canopy of the main marquee, surrounded by a
makeshift racetrack.

Danny and Matthew helped Grandad Nobby
carry his enormous vegetables into the marquee,
where the judging would take place later. Tables
ran around the edge, all covered in clean, crisp
white cloths. They were
crammed with vegetables
of all shapes and sizes,
arranged either neatly
in little piles, or
as large, single
specimens. The
table carrying

Grandad's massive marrow, beautiful beans and cracking carrots bowed in the middle with their weight.

Grandad placed a small card with his name on in front of them. He beamed with pleasure.

'You're going to win for sure, Grandad,' said Danny.

At that moment Ernie Slack strode towards them, dragging with him the Chief Judge, Mr Willis. Ernie was as long, thin and stringy as one of Grandad's runner beans, and his long, thin, stringy black moustache curled at each end like a pig's tail.

'You must disqualify Nobby Baker this instant!' he demanded. 'Those vegetables aren't normal – he's cheating!'

Judge Willis raised an eyebrow. 'They're certainly extraordinary, Ernie. But I can't see any reason to disqualify Nobby.'

Ernie blustered and fumed, and the ends of his curly moustache twitched with temper, but Danny could see that he knew Judge Willis was right. Ernie Slack stomped away.

Grandad grinned and turned to the boys. 'The judging's this afternoon, right after the Puddlethorpe Grand National,'  he said. He handed them five pounds each. 'You lads go and enjoy yourselves.'

Danny and Matthew thanked Grandad and went out into the bright late-summer sunshine. The hubbub of the crowd mixed with the bleating of sheep and the lowing of cows. The boys bought a hot dog each, listened to the Puddlethorpe Cowbell Ringers, and then tried out the fun and games. Danny managed to Dunk the Vicar, and won a pen shaped like a turnip. Matthew had had so much practice zapping worms that morning that he easily took first prize in the Junior Cowpat-Hurling Competition, and won a gold medallion in the shape of a cowpat.

'Ace!' said Danny.

'Cool!' agreed Matthew as they compared prizes.

Soon, everyone at the Fair began to gather for the main event of the afternoon: the Puddlethorpe Grand National. Six pantomime horses, each made up of two people and carrying a scarecrow jockey, lined up to race around a course that circled the main marquee. Danny spotted Grandma and Grandad in the crowd, and the boys pushed through to join them.

Tom Abson's voice boomed out over a loudspeaker in the centre of the field. 'Welcome to the thirty-eighth year of our famous race. The runners and riders are ready. Keep your eye on last year's winner, Ee By Gum, in the pink.'

The crowd began to cheer, calling out the names of their favourite horses. The referee held his starting pistol in the air and with a loud *CRACK!* the race began.

'And they're off!' yelled Tom Abson. 'There's a lot of bumping and banging going on as they

jockey for position coming up to the first hurdle . . .
Whoops-a-daisy . . .'

Three horses tumbled at the fence, where they
lay struggling and tangled up on the grass. Ee By
Gum and Ecky Thump went over safely.

The commentary continued. 'Coming up to the
next hurdle, and Ee By Gum's over, Ecky Thump's
over . . . Oh no! What a Load of Baloney is down
and he's lost his head! Don't look children, it's
horrible!'

Ee By Gum and Ecky Thump raced neck and neck
around the rest of the course. It was still close going
over the final hurdle, but then Ee By Gum jumped
two feet in the air and began to twitch and kick.

'There's something
wrong inside Ee By Gum,'
declared Tom Abson. 'If
I'm not mistaken, it
looks like they've got a
bee on board.'

Suddenly, Ee By Gum
went off course, charged into

Ecky Thump and bowled over several spectators.
The pantomime horse bucked and pranced across
the winning line as the two men inside were stung
by the bee.

The crowd cheered and clapped. People at
the back craned their necks to get
a better look. Danny turned to
say something to Matthew,
and the smile dropped from
his face. Over his friend's
shoulder, Danny saw Ernie
Slack sneaking into the empty
marquee, wielding a huge axe.

'Grandad!' he yelled.

'Stop him!' shouted
Grandad, but no one heard
his voice above the noise of the
crowd roaring at the pantomime horses. The boys
began to force their way through the press of people
behind them, to get to the marquee.

'It's no good,' said Danny. 'We'll never get there
in time!'

# Stinky

The loudspeakers set around the field let out a loud wet coughing sound that silenced the crowd.

'What's that awful pong?' spluttered Tom Abson. 'It's like boiled cabbage and seaweed and eggs and cheese and drains all mixed together.'

'My Rotting Chowhabunga!' cried Grandad. 'The flower must have opened!'

The animals in pens near the marquee became agitated.

The sheep went 'Moo'.

The cows went 'Baa'.

The geese went 'Woof'.

The pigs didn't seem bothered at all.

People fled, holding their noses in disgust. The stink was truly terrible.

Danny spied a hardware stall nearby, and grabbed a handful of wooden pegs.

'This worked when I had toxic toes,' he explained. He clipped one on to his nose, and handed out the others.

Pegs in place, Grandad, Grandma and the boys hurried into the marquee. A shocking sight met their eyes: Ernie Slack stood over Grandad's marrow, the axe raised high above his head, ready to strike.

'No!' yelled Grandad. 'Stop!'

But Ernie Slack *had* stopped. He was as stiff as a statue.

The big pot containing the Rotting Chowhabunga plant stood on a table in the centre of the marquee. The thick, purple star-shaped flower was open, and looked like a hand reaching up to the sky.

'The story was true!' said Grandad.

'Ace!' cried Danny.

'Cool!' agreed Matthew.

The boys ran forward. 'Has he *really* been turned into stone?' Matthew wondered.

Danny prodded Ernie Slack's tummy and it wobbled a little. 'No,' he replied, disappointed. 'He's just sort of . . . frozen.'

'You'd better take some photos of your flower before it dies,' suggested Grandma.

'Aye, I will,' replied Grandad. 'But first I'm going to get evidence.' He pulled a camera out of his pocket, and took photographs of Ernie Slack about to do his dastardly deed.

'Boys, go and find Judge Willis,' said Grandma. 'Tell him to put a peg on his nose and come quick. He needs to see this.'

Danny and Matthew returned with Judge Willis, and while the grown-ups tutted and shook their heads at the frozen cheat, the boys picked up the pot containing the Rotting Chowhabunga and heaved it out of the big tent. They carried it to the far end of the field, and placed it under an old pear tree.

'It shouldn't do any harm over here,' said Danny.

Immediately four calling birds, three French hens, two turtle doves and a partridge plummeted senseless from the branches of the pear tree on to the grass below.

'This *must* be the stinkiest flower in the world,' said Danny.

'It's awesome,' admired Matthew. 'Not as bad as your feet though.'

'No,' agreed Danny. 'Not *that* bad.'

When they got back to the main marquee, the paralysing effect of the Rotting Chowhabunga's stink had worn off, and Ernie Slack had thawed out. He stood like a naughty schoolboy before Judge Willis and the huge crowd of spectators.

'Because of your unsportsmanlike behaviour, you are disqualified from this year's competition,' the judge said sternly. He reached into the top pocket of his jacket and brandished a red card.

Ernie's face darkened, like a little thunder cloud about to burst, and his curly black moustache nearly twitched off his face. The crowd booed and hissed as he slunk from the marquee.

Judge Willis held up his hand and everyone fell silent. 'Ladies and gentlemen, let the judging begin!'

It was an agonizing wait, as the judges judged. One by one, they pronounced the winners of the Spottiest Cow, the Pig with the Curliest Tail, the Sheep with the Loudest Baa, the Sweetest Rose, the Sunniest Marigold, the Crustiest Loaf, the Most Tear-jerking Onion . . .

At last Judge Willis declared, 'The winner of First Prize for Most Massive Marrow in Show goes to . . . Nobby Baker!'

'Yessssssssssssssssssss!' cried Grandad, Grandma, Danny and Matthew together.

Grandad also won Blue Rosettes for the Longest Carrot and Stringiest Beans. Finally Judge Willis announced, 'We have one extra-special award to give, one that we have never awarded before and I hope will never *ever* award again. The prize for the Stinkiest Flower in Show goes to Nobby Baker!'

Everyone clapped and cheered. Grandad beamed with joy.

When the award ceremony was over, the judges came to shake hands with Grandad.

'So, Nobby, what's the special ingredient you've been feeding your vegetables with this year?' asked Judge Willis. Grandad tapped the side of his nose with his finger. 'It's a secret.' He smiled.

'A *super* secret!' exclaimed Danny and Matthew.

'I just wish I knew what the super secret was,' admitted Grandad when the judge had gone.

# Nobby Baker - Record Breaker

Crag Top Farm
Puddlethorpe

Dear Mr Bibby

For once I'm not asking about a
record for me, I'm writing about
my grandad, Nobby. Yesterday at the
Puddlethorpe Annual Country Fair his
Rotting Chowhabunga plant finally flowered for
the very first time. It was the stinkiest flower
I've ever smelt.

Grandad

Grandad says that this is
the first time a Rotting
Chowhabunga has ever
flowered in captivity. Is this

TOXIC!

Phewee

245

true, and does that make my grandad a record breaker?

Best wishes
Danny Baker

PS I've sent a picture of the flower to prove he did it. It's lucky for you I didn't take it with a Smello-vision camera!

Totally <u>stinky</u> ↗

The Great Big Book
of World Records
London

THE
★GREAT★
BIG
★BOOK OF★
★WORLD★
RECORDS

ARE YOU A RECORD
BREAKER?

Dear Danny,

Thank you for your letter. Actually, I *have* smelt the Rotting Chowhabunga flower. I once went to the Amazon jungle just to smell it. The local people know when the flower is about to open, because the forest clears of animals just before it happens. Flocks of birds rise from the trees and troupes of monkeys flee in panic. The smell reminded me of boiled cabbage and seaweed and eggs and cheese and drains all mixed together. Because of the legend, I was careful not to get too close, but even at a distance of fifteen metres my nose went numb and my toes began to tingle! I'm very glad I wasn't in that marquee at the Fair when the flower opened.

I have checked all my records and it's true:

this is the first time the Rotting Chowhabunga
has been made to flower outside the jungles
of Brazil. Your grandad *is* a record breaker,
and it gives me great pleasure to enclose his
certificate.

Best wishes,
Eric Bibby
Keeper of the Records

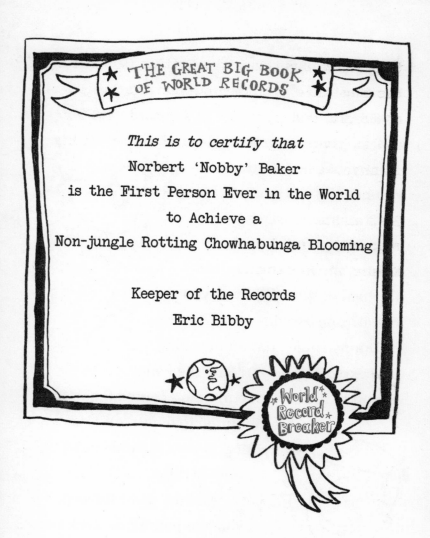

**THE GREAT BIG BOOK OF WORLD RECORDS**

*This is to certify that*
Norbert 'Nobby' Baker
is the First Person Ever in the World
to Achieve a
Non-jungle Rotting Chowhabunga Blooming

Keeper of the Records
Eric Bibby

World Record Breaker

'Do you mind me getting one of these instead of you, Danny?' asked Grandad.

'No, 'course not,' replied Danny. 'We had loads of fun helping you win it.'

Grandma glanced up from the little pink baby bonnet she was knitting, and frowned at him. 'What do you mean?' she asked.

Danny smiled a naughty smile, and explained how adding the Pongy Potion to the cowpat barrel had caused the Rotting Chowhabunga to flower, and made everything in the vegetable patch grow so huge.

'And the great thing is, you can beat Ernie Slack *every* year!' said Danny.

Matthew held up a piece of paper. 'Because I wrote down

the Pongy Potion recipe!'

Grandma put down her knitting and looked at the list Matthew had made. 'You used my home-made baked beans!' she complained.

Danny tapped the side of his nose. '*They* must have been the Super-Secret Ingredient!' he said.

# A NOTE FROM THE AUTHOR

# The Wibbly Wobbly Jelly Belly Flop

# A Smashing Attempt

To the Keeper of the Records
The Great Big Book of World Records
London


Dear Mr Bibby


My head teacher, Mr
Rogers, has banned me
from doing world records
at school again. It was
lunchtime and I was trying
to break the record for
carrying dirty dishes, but I
ended up breaking 24 bowls, 8 glasses and an egg
cup instead!


My best friend, Matthew, had stacked 12 bowls
along each of my arms in piles of two, with

banana split

spoons wedged in between and glasses balanced on each bowl. It was going well until I slipped on a big dollop of banana split, and went flying.

Mandy Badegg, a girl in my class, ended up with a gooey bowl on her head, and my teacher, Mrs Woodcock, got bopped on the bum by a flying spoon. They weren't happy. Four glasses landed upright on the table and caught falling spoons in them – Mega Ace! The dishes and the rest of the glasses hit the floor and smashed into a trillion sticky pieces. The dinner ladies weren't happy either.

Mandy

Mrs Woodcock

Bum

Matt measured the distance I walked before I

slipped at 19.63 metres. I don't suppose this is far enough to break the record, but I thought I'd ask.

Best wishes
Danny Baker

PS The Penleydale Safety Police have banned dishes and glasses and knives and forks from our school, because they say they're too dangerous. We've got to drink from plastic cups and eat off paper plates with our fingers. Munching rhubarb crumble and custard without a spoon will be mega gross! I can't wait!

Dear Danny

Manual Used-crockery Conveyance ('Dish-
carrying') is a skill that requires years of
practice.

One man stands above the rest. Italian Franco
Gennaro holds the world records for Single
Arm, Double Arm, and Whole Body Manual Used-
crockery Conveyance. In all his years of waiting
on tables, Franco has never dropped a single
item. He will clear tables by holding spoons in
his mouth, knives and forks behind his ears,
and uneaten bread rolls in his armpits. On
20 July 2007 Franco safely carried, from the
restaurant to the kitchen, 103 full-sized dinner
plates, 103 small side plates, and 309 pieces of
cutlery a distance of 34.97 metres. He smashed

his own record (but not the plates!) with ease.

Bad luck on your latest attempt, Danny. I hope
you didn't hurt yourself when you slipped!

Best wishes
Eric Bibby
Keeper of the Records

It was sports day at Coalclough Primary School. The place buzzed with activity and excitement. The sun was shining, the Big Field had just been mown, and the summery scent of freshly cut grass mingled with the delicious aroma of sausage rolls and pizzas cooking in the school kitchens.

Everyone was outside getting things ready for the afternoon's events: untangling skipping ropes, putting boiled eggs and spoons together, and setting out rows of chairs along each side of the straight running track for the spectators.

Danny and Matthew were doing some last-minute practice for the three-legged race. Every few paces they tumbled over and lay on the ground in a fit of giggles as they struggled to get on their feet again.

Suddenly a shrill, icy voice pierced the warm summer air.

'Not on your nelly!'

The children and teachers froze.

'This is *outrageous*!' bellowed the voice. 'This is *unsafe*!'

Danny looked round to see a huge barrel-shaped woman striding across the grass towards them. She wore an orange overall, a crash helmet on her head, safety goggles over her eyes, thick rubber gloves on her hands, and black protective pads on her knees. She trundled through a gaggle of startled children like a huge orange bowling ball, scattering them like skittles.

'I am Mrs Meaney, Chief of the Safety Police,' she announced, glaring at Danny and Matthew. 'You stupid boys could tumble and break your legs! The three-legged race is banned!'

The woman pointed a quivering finger at the goalposts at one end of the field. 'And what is *that* for?'

'It's for the penalty shoot-out competition,' said Danny. 'I'm in goal, and everyone has to try to score past me.'

'Not on your nelly! You could stub your toe kicking the ball! You could crack your ribs diving on to the hard ground! The penalty shoot-out is banned!'

Her fierce eyes scanned the field. 'It's a good thing I was tipped off about this,' she said, pointing at the various objects set up for each event.

'Skipping! You could trip and break your ankles! Banned!

'Sack races! You could crash and break your skull! Banned!

'Egg-and-spoon races! You could stumble and break your wrists! Banned!

'Tug of war! You could slip and break your bottoms! Banned!'

Mrs Meaney gasped as she picked up a 'First Place' certificate. She pointed at the edge of the thin card. 'This paper is sharper than a knife blade. It could slice your thumb off! Banned!'

'But we've been planning sports day for weeks,' said Matthew. 'All our families are coming to watch. It has to go ahead!'

'Not on your nelly!' replied Mrs Meaney. 'Sports day. Banned!'

'Party pooper,' whispered Danny.

'Spoilsport,' agreed Matthew under his breath.

'Think of some *safe* events to do,' said the safety chief. 'Like . . . making daisy chains.'

Danny snorted. 'But if you got a *really* tough daisy you could break your finger trying to pick it,' he said.

Mrs Meaney looked shocked. 'You're right!' she gasped. 'Daisy chains! Banned!'

# Magic Maths

Dear Mr Bibby

It's not fair! Mrs Meaney from the safety police cancelled our school sports day because she said all the games were too dangerous! Me and Matt decided to protest by trying to break a record from one of the banned games.

Mrs Meaney

We tied our legs together and did the three-legged race. (Actually, it wasn't a proper race because we were the only ones running.) We kept

me and Matt

falling over at first, but the more we practised, the better we got. On our last run we covered 50 metres in 26.44 seconds and only fell over once. Did we break the record?

Best wishes
Danny Baker

PS We're not going to let Mrs Meaney stop us having fun. We're going to fight back and find a way to have our competition after all. We're just not sure how.

The Great Big Book
of World Records
London

ARE YOU A RECORD
BREAKER ?

Dear Danny

I'm sorry, but your time for Artificially
Joined Tri-legged Sprinting (to give the three-
legged race its official title) was a good deal
slower than the world record. This is held by
brothers Bill and Ben Bullitt from Barbados
who, on 17 December last year, three-legged it
over 50 metres in a blistering 7.23 seconds.

Until then, all records for this sport were
held by husband and wife team Rudi and Trudi
Loof of Sweden. They were unbeatable, until
they tripped and fell in a race last October
in Stuttgart, spraining Rudi's ankle. When
doctors examined him, they discovered that Rudi
actually had *three* legs! His 'wife' Trudi was,
in fact, a one-legged shop-window dummy that

**269**

he had strapped to his
waist. As you can see
from the attached photo,
I'm amazed nobody
realized!

Rudi and Trudi (Stuttgart)

The Artificially
Joined Tri-legged
Sprinting Association
took a dim view of
his cheating. Rudi was banned
for life and stripped of all his world records.

It's a shame that your sports day was
cancelled, but if I know you, Danny, you'll find
a solution.

Best wishes
Eric Bibby
Keeper of the Records

'Beaky' Rogers, the Coalclough Primary School head teacher, came in to talk to Danny's class.

'I know you are all disappointed about sports day,' he began, 'but I have some great news to cheer you up. In two weeks' time, the twenty-fifth annual Making Maths Magic! event will be held in Penleydale. Schools from twelve countries will be taking part in five days of numeracy fun! I am tremendously proud to announce that this class will be representing our school *and* Great Britain!'

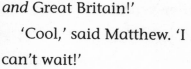

'Cool,' said Matthew. 'I can't wait!'

'You're weird, Matt,' said Danny. 'I'd rather have sports-day fun, and I'm not giving up on it. The safety police aren't going to beat *me*.'

\*

At break, the boys had fun trying to make up 'safe' events that Mrs Meaney couldn't possibly object to.

'Puddle Splashing?' suggested Danny.

'Maybe,' said Matthew. 'As long as the puddles aren't too deep.'

'Biscuit Dunking . . .'

'Yeah! As long as the tea isn't too hot.'

'Pillow Fighting . . .'

'As long as the pillows aren't too hard,' said Matthew.

'The Low Jump!' said Danny. 'The Short Jump! The Triple Bunny Jump!'

'How about a Ten-metre Slow-motion Race?' suggested Matthew. 'The winner is the person who comes last!'

Danny's eyes stretched wide as an idea popped into his head. 'The Wibbly Wobbly Jelly Belly Flop! Diving into jelly! I'd love to do *that*! And who could hurt themselves on some squidgy jelly?'

'It would definitely be the *safest* sports day ever,' laughed Matthew, scribbling the new ideas at the end of the list.

'And the silliest!' said Danny. 'Let's do it! I'll organize a load of daft games, and you can organize all the measuring and timing and scoring.'

'What if we made it part of the Making Maths Magic! event?' said Matthew. 'We could do the events during the day, and then in the evening use the results to work out speeds, distances, averages, ratios, fractions, percentages and ranking tables. That way, we can have sports day *and* make numeracy fun!'

'Countries from around the world competing . . .' mused Danny. 'We could call it the "*Silly* Olympics"!'

'Let's talk to Beaky Rogers,' said Matthew. 'And see if he'll let us do it.'

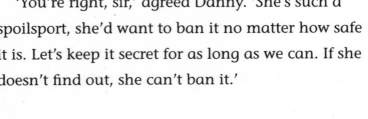

At lunchtime, the boys explained their plan to the head teacher.

'It'd be a really fun way to learn maths,' said Matthew.

'And we'll organize everything,' added Danny.

'It's an excellent idea, boys,' said Mr Rogers, studying the list of events. 'But Mrs Meaney won't like it.'

'You're right, sir,' agreed Danny. 'She's such a spoilsport, she'd want to ban it no matter how safe it is. Let's keep it secret for as long as we can. If she doesn't find out, she can't ban it.'

The head teacher stared thoughtfully at the boys down his long beaky nose. 'Let me think about it,' he said.

After school, the boys made their way to Penley Park for a kick about. They strolled past the bandstand and headed towards the towering horse chestnut in the centre of the park, known as the Duelling Tree. A local legend said that the tree had sprouted from the triumphant conker planted in 1723 by the third Earl of Penley, after beating the dastardly French Duke Antoine de Guillotine in a conker duel.

Tall spikes of flowers, like chunky white candles, smothered the spreading branches.

'Wow!' said Danny. 'We're going to get trillions of conkers this year. Ace!'

'What's this?' asked Matthew, pointing at a dripping red cross slashed in paint on the trunk. There was a sign nailed to the tree above it. 'She's spoiling everything!' groaned Matthew.

Danny glared at the sign. 'We've got to stop her.'

'I think she's unstoppable,' said Matthew.

'Don't worry,' said Danny. 'We'll think of something.'

# Pass It On

Dear Mr Bibby

Me and Matthew have been given the go-ahead to organize the world's first Silly Olympics in Penleydale!

All the schools that are coming to the Making Maths Magic! marathon are going to join in too. We started a Pass It On that went from one school to another in 12 countries, right around the world:

Albania to Papua New Guinea

India to Greenland

Papua New Guinea to Madagascar

Mexico to Belarus

Greenland to Peru

Canada to India

Great Britain to Mexico

Belarus to Canada

Peru to New Zealand

Madagascar to Japan

New Zealand to Albania

Japan Back to Great Britain

Has there ever been a Pass It On that went right around the world?

The games begin a week on Monday. Could you come as Guest of Honour and present the medals? It would be Mega Ace to meet you at last. Mum and Dad said that you can stay at our house and sleep in my room — I'll be camping with Matt in a tent at the Kids' Camp!

Best wishes
Danny Baker
Director of Events, Silly Olympics

PS We're trying to keep it a secret from the World's Biggest Spoilsport, Mrs Meaney of the safety police — she'd only go and spoil the fun!

The Great Big Book
of World Records
London

Dear Danny

Thank you very much for inviting me to
attend the world's first Silly Olympics! It
would be an honour to be there. I'm going to
Australia next week to check for records at
the World Boomerang-balancing championships,
but luckily I get back to England the day
before your Silly Olympics begins. I look
forward to lots of new world records being
broken.

The Chinese Whisper ('Pass It On') that spread
the word about the games was not a world
beater, I'm afraid. In 2004, thirteen-year-old
Kieran Puffett of Green Spot, Arizona, USA,
organized a surprise fortieth birthday party
for his mother at their house. He asked friends

and relatives to 'pass it on', but things got
horribly out of control.

The message eventually reached his mum's
second cousin, Tammy Fender, who worked at
NASA, the space agency. She accidentally beamed
Kieran's message into space, where it bounced
off satellites orbiting the earth and appeared
simultaneously on televisions all over the
globe. As a result, 326,103 people from 188
different countries turned up to the party,
making it not only the Biggest Pass It On,
but also the Biggest Fortieth Birthday Party
ever!

Kieran's mother was a bit cross when all these
guests arrived at her house. She was even more
cross that, thanks to Kieran, the whole world
knew she was forty years old. She grounded him
for three months.

Let's hope the same thing doesn't happen to

you, Danny! Good luck organizing the Silly
Olympics - I can't wait!

Eric Bibby
Keeper of the Records

PS I won't tell a soul about the games -
*especially* not Mrs Meaney!

Danny and Matthew worked hard to make sure
that everything would be ready on time. The
evening before all the other school teams were due
to fly in to Walchester Airport, the boys stood high
in the Donkey Lane Stand of Penleydale Town's
football ground. They gazed across a sea of bright
red tents, clustered into twelve groups around
the flag of each country taking part in the Silly
Olympics. A huge white marquee had been erected
in the centre of the pitch, where all the results
calculations and maths lessons would take place.

The smell of warm pies and sizzling sausages
wafted up from the Plumpton's Pie and Pea Shop,

and the Hungry Hound Hotdog Stall. They were cooking supper for all the volunteers bustling around the ground, and would also provide the calorie-controlled, vitamin-enriched athlete's diet the children needed during the games.

The boys ran through the checklist on Matthew's clipboard one last time.

VENUES and EVENTS

Ready?

Penleydale Town FC
- Kids' Camp - tents, food, showers toilets ⟶  ✓
- Making Maths Magic! Marquee

Penley Park
- Hat Flinging  ✓
- Umbrella Twirling
- Blindfold Leapfrogging  ✓
- Custard-pie Discus
- 10-metre Slow-motion Race
- Boxing-glove Baked-bean Pick-up
- Syncronized Crumpet-buttering  ✓
- Balloon Keepy-Uppies

Farmer Shufflebottom's maize field at Mop Top Farm
- Maize Maze Marathon

Penleydale Pool (the 'Splatterdrome')
- Butterfly-swimming in Blancmange
- 15-metre flipper-dash in yogurt
- Wibby wobbly Jelly Belly flop

'We've *definitely* got to keep this secret from Mrs Meaney,' said Matthew. 'She'd never let us get away with Blindfold Leapfrogging.'

'She wouldn't let us do *any* of it,' said Danny. He mimicked the safety-police chief. 'Balloons? They could pop and break your ears! Banned!'

'Let's go over the equipment,' laughed Matthew, flipping on to the next page of his clipboard. 'Twenty gold, twenty silver and twenty bronze chocolate medals . . . that's way too many!'

Danny grinned. 'We'll eat what's left over.'

'Check!' agreed Matthew.

'Medal table?'

'Just waiting for the paint to dry – check.'

'Stopwatches, tape measures, whistles . . .'

'Check, check, check!' said Matthew, ticking all the boxes. He took a deep breath and blew it out slowly as he scanned the list. 'We must've forgotten *something*.'

'If we have, it's too late now,' said Danny. 'Come on, I want my pie and peas!'

*

When Danny got home, his tummy was fizzing with excitement for the start of the games. However, his good mood was soon smashed to pieces.

'Why do I have to sleep in Natalie's room?' he asked, standing at his sister's bedroom door and holding his nose to keep out the sweet girlie smell of flowers.

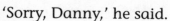

Dad patted Danny's shoulder sympathetically.

'Sorry, Danny,' he said. 'Mum wants to clean your room before Mr Bibby comes to stay. It's only for one night, then you can move to the Kids' Camp with all the other children.'

Danny's sleeping bag lay on the pink carpet next to the pink chair in the far corner of the room. A long strip of pink ribbon was tied from the door to the chair, dividing the room in two. A sign hanging on the ribbon ordered: KEEP OUT! OR ELSE!

Natalie stomped over and thrust a piece of paper at Danny.

1. NO entry without the password: Natalie is beautiful
2. NO muddy shoes
3. NO messy clothes →
4. NO smelly socks →
5. NO dirty underpants
6. NO creepy-crawlies →
7. NO TRUMPING! →

'Stay in your corner, obey the rules, or I'll turn you into mashed potato,' said Natalie.

Danny sighed and stepped into the room. His

sister stopped him and pointed to rule number 1 on the paper.

Danny sighed again. 'Natalie is beautiful,' he said.

'I know,' she smiled. 'You may enter!'

Danny trudged over to his sleeping bag.

'What's that revolting smell?' cried Natalie, her face crumpling with disgust.

'Kippers!' explained Danny, rummaging in his bag and pulling out two rotten stinky fish. 'I've got to slap my tummy with them three times a day – it's what professional belly floppers do.'

He hitched up his T-shirt and demonstrated.

'Mum!' yelled Natalie. 'Tell him!'

Danny didn't get much sleep that night, thanks to

Natalie's rasping snores. He couldn't stop yawning as he and Matthew made their way to the Kids' Camp the next morning.

They wanted to get there early to welcome the other schools from around the world as they arrived.

'Are you wearing perfume?' asked Matthew, sniffing his friend.

'No!' protested Danny. 'Nat said my sleeping bag ponged of boys, so she sprayed it with some stinky stuff called "Romance". I got my own back though – *her* bed smelt of girls, so I gave it a rub down with one of my whiffy kippers!'

The boys were busy all day, directing new arrivals to tents, toilets, showers and food stalls, and handing out special T-shirts printed with each country's flag.

Matthew had put a list of all the events on a table. It quickly filled up with names, as children signed up to the ones they wanted to take part in. Some children volunteered to help out as judges and timekeepers when they weren't competing.

'Ace!' said Danny, as he examined the long list of names under each event. 'It looks like everyone wants to have a go at everything! We'll have to have qualifying heats, then semi-finals, before the *final* final!'

He picked up a pen and added his name for the last event of the Silly Olympics: the Wibbly Wobbly Jelly Belly Flop.

'I'm not entering anything,' said Matthew. 'I'll just have fun doing the maths.'

Danny shook his head. 'You're really weird, Matt.'

By the time the welcome barbecue and campfire sing-song began, there was a party atmosphere in the stadium. The grown-ups kept telling everyone to 'sit down!', 'be careful!', 'don't run!' and 'be quiet!'.

'These maths teachers are a nuisance,' grumbled Matthew. 'They're going to spoil the games more than Mrs Meaney would.'

'We need to get rid of them somehow,' agreed Danny.

Matthew thought for a moment, and then smiled. 'Leave it to me.'

# Let the Silliness Begin!

Next morning, Danny and Matthew rushed around the Kids' Camp, struggling to organize the parade to Penley Park marking the beginning of the Silly Olympics. Just like the day before, teachers kept spoiling the fun, bossing people around and laying down rules.

'Line up there,' ordered Mrs Woodcock. 'And put those flags down!'

'No, line up here!' said Danny. 'And hold those flags high!'

'Don't worry,' whispered Matthew. 'I've got a cool Teacher Removal Plan to get them out of the way.'

'Can you see anyone who might be Mr Bibby?' asked Danny, scanning the camp to see if the Keeper of the Records had arrived. 'I don't know what he looks like.'

'Maybe he's gone straight to the park,' replied Matthew.

At last, the athletes gathered into their teams and everyone was ready to go. Matthew had been given the honour of marching at the front of the British children. As Director of Events, Danny was to lead the whole parade.

Matthew looked his friend up and down. 'You need a big badge, or a fancy hat like the Lord Mayor wears,' he said. 'Something that tells people you're in charge.'

'Like what?' said Danny. He searched around and spied a single sad sausage lying cold and wrinkled on the grill from last night's barbecue. He stabbed it with a fork, struck a noble pose and held the banger high above his head.

'The Silly Sausage!' he declared, marching out of the camp towards Penley Park.

The other children let out a massive cheer and followed him.

As Danny led the parade through the town, it seemed as if the whole of Penleydale lined the streets, waving and clapping as the children marched past.

He had been so busy organizing the events, Danny hadn't seen what his schoolmates had done to decorate Penley Park. As he strode through the gates, a tingle of excitement raced through his body.

Trees were festooned with sparkling silver streamers, which twinkled magically in the afternoon sunshine. Multicoloured bunting criss-crossed the sky above the children, stretched between street lights and bandstand.

As Danny approached the Duelling Tree, he gasped. Mrs Meaney's red cross had been scrubbed from the bark and the sign removed. Tiny flags of all the nations taking part in the Silly Olympics fluttered happily among the leaves, and from a distance the whole tree shimmered like a mirage.

Danny turned to Matthew. 'The safety police wouldn't dare cut it down now,' he said.

'Wouldn't they?' replied his friend.

One by one, the twelve teams of children gathered before the tree, filling up the flat expanse of grass in the centre of the park that was now the Silly Sports Arena. Straight white lines in the middle marked out a short running track, and areas around it were sectioned off for the other events.

A noisy crowd of spectators surrounded them, cheering as each team took its place. The Coalclough Primary School Pots and Pans Orchestra played jaunty, clinky-clanky tunes, while the Tippy-toes Cheerleading Team waved their multicoloured pompoms in the air, and kicked and jiggled and whooped and whistled.

Mrs Meaney had banned fireworks last November, so at a sign from Danny the children began to blow soap bubbles into the air. In seconds, thousands of flimsy, shining rainbow-coloured bubbles swirled and popped above the park.

Just then, Danny's mum and dad hurried over.

'Where's Mr Bibby?' asked Danny.

'He's here . . . but he's not here,' replied Mum.

'He arrived this morning, and I was just showing him to your room when something very strange happened. He began to yawn and yawn and yawn. Then huge purple blotches erupted on his face and hands, his ears went droopy and he lost his voice! I was going to send for the doctor, but Mr Bibby knew what it was straight away.'

She showed Danny a neat handwritten note:

Don't panic, Mrs Baker! I've got Tasmanian Topsy-turvy Blotchyosity. I've just come back from Australia, and it's spreading like wildfire down there. It lasts about four days, but is very infectious, so I'll have to stay locked in Danny's room until it goes. Unfortunately, I'll be asleep all day and awake all night – just as though I was still on Australian time! I'm so

'Then he fell asleep, still holding on to his pen,' said Mum.

'But he's our Guest of Honour! He's supposed to open the Silly Olympics!' said Danny.

'This was your idea,' said Dad. 'Why don't *you* do it?'

'Me?' said Danny, staring out at the crowds packed into the park. 'Ace!'

Dad heaved Danny off the ground and on to his shoulders so that he could be seen by everyone. Danny held the Silly Sausage above his head.

'Ladies, gentlemen and children of the world,' he shouted. 'The safety police said it wouldn't happen. *We* said it would. Let the silliness begin!'

A massive cheer went up. Danny held his hand up quickly and everyone was silent once more.

'Hush!' he added. 'Don't tell Mrs Meaney!'

# Cheat

That evening, Mum left Mr Bibby's breakfast on a tray outside his bedroom door. Danny popped a letter in the toast rack, and then set off with Dad back to the Kids' Camp.

Dear Mr Bibby

The Silly Olympics is under way! We started with the qualifying heats for Umbrella Twirling. The kids from Mawsynram in India were brilliant twirlers – I can't see anyone stopping one of them from taking gold.

umbrella twirling

The 10-metre Slow-motion qualifying races were super-slow! Two of my classmates, Harry Dawkins and Amy Johnson, both got through to the semi-finals.

We awarded our first chocolate medals too, for Balloon Keepy-uppies and Hat Hurling.

Balloon Keepy-uppies is definitely an indoor sport! It was a bit windy this afternoon and the balloons got blown all over the park! It was super-silly. In the end, Yumi Yamamoto from Japan won the gold medal. Even though he only managed three keepy-uppies, he was still the best of the bunch!

The wind helped the Hat Hurlers though. The children from Zumpango in Mexico were Mega Ace – they took gold, silver and bronze! The winner, Pablo Gonzales, spun his sombrero so high into the air that the wind took it out of the park and right out of town. Farmer

Shufflebottom's got a
scarecrow in the middle of
his maize maze, and
Pablo's sombrero
came down right on
its head – what a
shot!

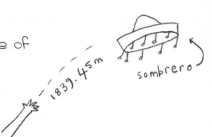

Matt measured the hat-hurl at a massive
1839.45 metres. Is this a record?

Best wishes
Danny
Director of Events, Silly Olympics

The following morning the boys were checking the Silly Sports Arena in Penley Park, making sure that everything was ready for the second day of the games. Danny had stuck the Silly Sausage behind his right ear, so that people would know he was in charge.

'Where are all the maths teachers?' he asked, noticing that the only grown-ups in the park were all the Volunteer Mums, who had been helping out with mealtimes and tidying up.

'They're in the Making Maths Magic! marquee back at camp, trying to work this out,' replied Matthew, handing Danny a piece of paper. 'I've called it Matt Mason's Mega Maths Conundrum.'

Written on the paper was the longest, hardest, craziest sum Danny had ever seen. His eyes watered and his head went woozy just looking at it. The numbers and symbols seemed to jumble and swim around the page.

'My brain hurts,' said Danny, handing the sum back to Matthew.

'The maths teachers will love it!' said his friend. 'They'll be in the marquee for days trying to work it out!'

'And out of our way! Ace!'

The boys high-fived. Dad strolled across the field and handed Danny a letter from Mr Bibby.

'Have you met him yet?' asked Danny.

'No,' replied Dad. 'I heard him going downstairs in the middle of the night to make his topsy-turvy lunch, but I don't want droopy ears and purple blotches, so I didn't go and say hello. He did the washing up and left that letter on the table.'

Dad wished them luck and set off for work. Danny opened the letter.

Dear Danny

Congratulations on getting the Silly Olympics started! I'm sorry we can't meet in person, but I really don't want you catching Tasmanian Topsy-turvy Blotchyosity. At least I can let you know very quickly if anyone has broken a record - I've set up a hotline to my headquarters in London, and I have your entire collection of *The Great Big Book of World Records* annuals to consult!

I'm not surprised the school from Mawsynram in India are brilliant Umbrella-Twirlers - they live in the wettest region on earth and have around 12 metres of rain every year! To them, leaving home without an umbrella is worse than going out with no trousers on!

Pablo's medal-winning Manual Headwear Propulsion (Hat-Hurling) effort was magnificent, but did not break the record. In fact, I doubt this record will ever be broken. In 2008, fellow

Mexican Eduardo Soto of El Salto flicked his special aero-dynamically designed sombrero into space! It was carried on an updraught of hot air caused by the eruption of the volcano Mount Mamasanpapas, and went into orbit around the earth. The adventurous hat was tracked by observatories around the globe. It only came to rest when it snagged on the nose of the space shuttle *Discovery* as it began its re-entry into the earth's atmosphere. Sadly Eduardo's sombrero was burned to a crisp, but not before it had travelled a distance of 32,392 kilometres!

Keep me updated on the performances, Danny. I'm sure someone will break a record soon.

Best wishes
Eric Bibby
Keeper of the Records

PS Your bedroom reminds me of my room when I was your age: full of interesting things!

Danny had just folded Mr Bibby's letter and stuffed it into his pocket, when there was a loud cry of 'Cheat!'.

The boys hurried over to where a small group of children was warming up to take part in the Custard-pie Discus. Pablo, the gold medal Hat Hurler from Mexico, was pointing angrily at Mandy Badegg, a girl in Danny's class. She was quivering like a jelly in a force-ten gale.

'This girl is cheating,' said Pablo, showing Danny and Matthew a plastic bag containing four empty bottles of fizzy pop, five doughnuts, three iced buns, and dozens of empty chewy-sweet wrappers.

'She's trying to get a sugar boost to help her win!' exclaimed Matthew.

Mandy had eaten so much sweet stuff, she was almost buzzing. She kept squeaking and squealing as she spoke. 'I thought they were – wahaaaay! – sugar-free buns,' she lied.

Danny realized that, as the organizer of the games, he would need to take charge of the situation. Everyone had to play fair. He removed the Silly Sausage from behind his ear and pointed it at Mandy.

'You'll have to pee in a pot, so Nurse Tompkins can check your sugar levels,' he said, taking Mandy by the

arm and leading her towards the first-aid tent.

Mandy snatched the plastic bag containing all her cakes and pop. 'Gross!' she yelled. 'There's no way I'm doing that!'

'Then you're disqualified!' said Danny. 'Your Silly Olympics is over!'

Mandy's twitching face contorted into a mask of sugar-fuelled rage. 'Grrrrrrrrrrrr! Not on your nelly!' she growled, glaring at the boys. 'I want a gold medal – woohoo! – and if you don't make sure I get one – wahaaay! – I'm going to tell my auntie.'

Danny frowned. 'What's your auntie got to do with it?'

Mandy's lips twisted into a cruel smile. 'Yippee! My Auntie Meaney's the Head of the Safety Police, and she'll ban your stupid games, just like sports day! Yay! Yay! Yay!'

'It was *you* who tipped her off!' said Danny. He clenched his fists and gritted his teeth. 'OK. You win. I'll enter you for the Maize Maze Marathon in Farmer Shufflebottom's maize field tomorrow.'

'Yeeeeee-haaaaaaaa! And how are you going to make sure I win?'

'I'll give you a map of the maze. It shows the route to the middle. You'll probably get there so fast you'll win gold *and* break a world record.'

Mandy smirked, then twitched and jiggled away. 'I knew you'd see sense. Whoopee!'

Matthew gasped. 'Danny! That's cheating!'

Danny grinned. 'Don't worry, I've got a plan.'

The rest of the day passed without a hitch as the boys tried to be everywhere at once. They checked that the volunteers were doing their jobs properly – recording measurements and times, collecting scores and directing people to the right part of the arena for their event.

Just like the previous day, a huge crowd was packed into the park. Families and townspeople cheered the children on. Many had come to see the messiest, most difficult competition of the day: the Boxing-glove Baked-bean Pick-up. Competitors had to pick beans from the sloppy pile and put them in a jam-jar, while wearing boxing gloves.

Danny took a quick break from directing the game to watch the Synchronized Crumpet-buttering event. Luba and Svetlana Babkin, two ballerinas from Belarus, held the spectators in awe as they buttered their crumpets with perfectly timed leaps and swirls and somersaults.

The final of the most popular competition had been saved until last: the Custard-pie Discus – flinging sticky pies at Volunteer Dads, scoring two points for hitting their arms or legs, five points for tummies, and ten points for a 'bullseye' in the face.

At the end of the second day's competition, everyone gathered in front of the Duelling Tree to watch 'Beaky' Rogers present the winners with their medals. As each child stepped on to the podium, the Pots and Pans Orchestra clinked and clanked the national anthem of that country.

Danny stared in alarm at the medal table standing nearby.

# Silly Olympics

## MEDAL TABLE: DAY TWO

|  | gold | Silver | bronze |
|---|---|---|---|
| INDIA | 1 | 1 | 1 |
| MEXICO | 1 | 1 | 1 |
| BELARUS | 1 | 0 | 1 |
| GREENLAND | 1 | 0 | 0 |
| JAPAN | 1 | 0 | 0 |
| MADAGASCAR | 1 | 0 | 0 |
| ALBANIA | 0 | 1 | 0 |
| CANADA | 0 | 1 | 0 |
| PAPUA NEW GUINEA | 0 | 1 | 0 |
| NEW ZEALAND | 0 | 0 | 1 |
| PERU | 0 | 0 | 1 |
| GREAT BRITAIN | 0 | 0 | 0 |

'We're last!' cried Danny. 'Not Ace!'

'Not cool,' agreed Matthew. 'I hope your jelly belly flopping's on top form – at this rate it'll be up to you to win a medal for Great Britain!'

Everyone made their way back to the Kids' Camp to Make Maths Magic! over a pie and pea supper, and to check the teachers were still being kept busy doing Matt's Mega Maths Conundrum. So far, none of them had worked out the answer.

'This is my favourite bit,' said Matthew, busily calculating the average number of baked beans picked up per minute per competitor.

Danny scratched his head as he tried to work out how slow the winner of the 10-metre Slow-mo Race had 'run'.

'Matt, you're *mega* weird,' he said, spooning in a third helping of mushy peas. 'The pie and peas is *my* favourite bit!'

# Get Lost!

That evening, Danny went home to deliver the day's results to Mr Bibby.

'I managed to catch the Slow-mo Final this morning,' said Mum as she made Mr Bibby's breakfast. 'It was really boring!'

'But safe,' laughed Danny. 'Even Mrs Meaney couldn't say *that* was dangerous.'

Danny carried the tray upstairs and put it outside Mr Bibby's door. As he slipped his latest letter underneath the glass of orange juice, Natalie ambushed him with a can of air freshener.

'I can't get the stink of you or your kippers out of my bedroom!' she wailed. 'You're disgusting! You should be banned!'

'Don't tell the safety police, or I *will* be!' laughed Danny, racing out of the front door before Natalie could pull his ears off.

He dived into the car, and Dad sped off to take him back to the Kids' Camp.

Dear Mr Bibby

The Silly Olympics is fantastic! Me and Matthew are running round like ants on a sugar rush – we're tired out! It's been worth it though – there were some Ace performances today.

Bitti Uqalik from Greenland won the Baked-bean Pick-up by a pile. She said they wear thick mittens most of the year where they live, so picking baked beans up with a boxing glove was no problem!

Bitti

Sahondra Rakotomalala from Madagascar won the 10-metre Slow-mo race in 1 hour, 28 minutes and 13.9 seconds. She told me that at home she hunts for the Fearful Fidgit Fish. The fish is really hard to catch, because the slightest movement in the water and –

"fidgit fish"

zoom! – it's gone. Sahondra moves so slowly she's the finest Fearful Fidgit Fisher in Madagascar.

But the funniest event today was the Custard-pie Discus – chucking pies at grown-ups! I was just wishing I'd chosen to do that instead of the Jelly

custard-pie discus

Belly Flop, but then the grown-ups started to fling the pies back! Everyone joined in, and we all had a massive custard-pie fight! Ace! We had to cancel the competition because we used all the pies in the battle.

Matt counted 223 people chucking custard pies. Was this a record?

I've enclosed a list of today's results. Are there any record breakers?

Best wishes
Danny
Director of Events, Silly Olympics

Dear Danny

I'm really enjoying my stay in your room. I'm
reading all your comics and football programmes,
and I've autographed your entire collection of *The
Great Big Book of World Records*.

There were some tremendous performances on
day two of the games, but sadly none of them
broke a record. I was hoping that I could award
one to Luba and Svetlana Babkin, from Belarus,
but last month the ISA (International Sporting
Authority) refused to recognize Synchronized
Crumpet-buttering as a sport, so I'm not allowed
to.

Sahondra Rakotomalala is clearly an extremely
talented slow-motion runner, but Paula Crawler
from Hopton Wafers in Shropshire is the
undisputed queen of Imperceptible Perambulation
(Slow-motion Running). She is known as 'The
Slu', and in May 2002 covered 10 metres in

3 days, 7 hours, 15 minutes and 0.8 seconds.

Paula is currently doing the London marathon in slow motion, carrying a bucket of slime that she dribbles behind her, leaving a sticky shining trail just like a real gastropod.

When I last checked, she had travelled 322 metres in 77 days, 19 hours and 31 minutes. At this rate, it will take her about 28 years to complete the course. As no one has been silly enough to do this before, Paula Crawler will definitely be a record breaker!

I wish I'd seen the custard-pie fight. It couldn't beat the Battle of Blooming Bighill, during the American Civil War in 1865, however. The fighting raged for so long that both sides ran out of ammunition. The 6,000 Union soldiers used their custard-pie ration to attack the defenceless Confederate Army, which fled under the blistering barrage of sloppy bombs. It was a turning point in the war. After the battle, rumour has it that President Lincoln declared, 'Freedom! Peace! And custard pies!'

Keep sending updates, Danny!

Best wishes
Eric Bibby
Keeper of the Records

Before the third day of the Silly Olympics began, Mandy Badegg came swaggering towards the boys, grinning as though she had just won the lottery. She looked like an overstuffed binbag, as her T-shirt and track pants bulged with oddly shaped bumps.

'Why are you so lumpy?' asked Matthew.

'Jam doughnuts and pop bottles!' she replied, winking at him. 'It's my secret sugar stash, although I don't expect to be in the maze *that* long. Is everything ready for my gold-medal-winning performance?' she smirked.

Danny glanced around to make sure no one was watching, then slipped a folded piece of paper to Mandy. She opened it quickly and saw a map of the Maize Maze with a red line zigzagging through it to the centre. Grinning triumphantly, she got on the bus waiting to take the competitors to Mop Top

Farm. Danny watched it trundle out of the school gates, then strolled back to Matthew.

'Are you sure Farmer Shufflebottom plants a completely new Maize Maze every year?' asked Matthew.

'Certain,' grinned Danny. 'I've given Mandy a map of *last* year's maze. She'll get lost after turning the first corner!'

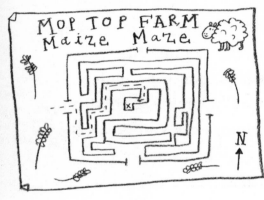

Danny spent the rest of the day hurrying between the gooey events at the 'Splatterdrome' and the remaining competitions at Penley Park.

He made sure he didn't miss the 15-metre Yogurt Flipper-dash qualifiers in the kiddies' pool. Competitors had to run through a pool of yogurt with swimming flippers on their feet. Just as Danny expected, it was a lot of silly, slippy-sloppy fun.

The Butterfly-swimming in Blancmange at the

Splatterdrome's
main pool wasn't
actually a race.
The winner was
the person who

could use the splishy-splashy
swimming stroke to splatter the most spectators
with sticky pudding. The event kept Matthew busy
all morning, measuring the 'slop-spread'.

'We're *definitely* in with a chance of winning
medals here,' he told Danny. 'Jimmy Sedgley's on
cracking splatter-form, and Gracie Green's neck-

and-neck for first
place in the
Flipper-dash.'
Danny
shook his
head. 'I'm
not so sure.
The girl from
New Zealand
lives on an

island and has to dash across the sand every day before the tide comes in, to get to school. She wears flippers in case she doesn't make it in time and has to swim the last few metres. I bet she steps up a gear in the final.'

The afternoon finished with the Blindfold Leapfrogging final in Penley Park.

Danny and Matthew met up at the end of the day for the medal ceremony in Penley Park.

'I've just seen the result of the Maize Maze Marathon,' said Matthew. 'Mandy didn't even finish. What if she sets her Auntie Meaney on us?'

'She can't,' replied Danny. 'She's still lost in the maze. We'll tell Farmer Shufflebottom to find her and let her out after supper. She'll be OK – she's got her sugary supplies to keep her going.'

When the children got back to the Kids' Camp, the teachers were still in the marquee trying to work out Matt's Mega Maths Conundrum.

Matthew smiled. 'They'll never work it out,' he whispered to Danny. 'It's impossible. I left out a couple of divide and multiply signs.'

'So Mandy's lost in the maize maze, and *they're* lost in a maths maze!' laughed Danny.

The boys high-fived.

'Matt, we're an a-*maze*-ing team!'

# A Big Flop!

Dear Mr Bibby

Another great day! We had an extra
competition in the park to make up for
cancelling the Custard-pie Discus — Paper-boat
Racing! It rained overnight, so
we had dozens of paper boats
being blown across puddles
all over the park. It
looked Ace — until most
of them got soggy and
sank. Three kids from the
Suki Swamp School in Papua New Guinea took gold,
silver and bronze!

*Paper boats!*

The Maize Maze Marathon was won by Billy
Knows Where He Is, from the Native American
Wherearewe tribe in Manitoba, Canada. He

Billy Knows Where He Is!

said they're called the Wherearewe tribe because they live in tangly tall grass over three metres high, and their ancestors used to wander around shouting, 'Where are we?' The kids there are used to working out twisty-turny paths through the grass to find their way to school, so the maze was easy-peasy for Billy.

I thought Blindfold Leapfrogging would be a mega-silly event that no one would be able to do without bumping into each other. I was right, except for two boys from Peru who made it look dead easy! Orlando Zender and Hartog Jumpa covered 50 metres in 15.7 seconds, and didn't fall over once!

50 metres

I've written out a list of winners from day three. One must be a record, surely?

Best wishes

Danny

Director of Events, Silly Olympics

PS It's the last day
tomorrow. I'll be competing
in the Wibbly Wobbly Jelly
Belly Flop — wish me luck!

my
jelly
belly!

Dear Danny

I'm sorry to say that no records were broken on day three either, but then there were some tough ones to beat.

The Suki people of Papua New Guinea spend most of their lives in boats on the great freshwater swamps there. They use paper boats to send messages to each other, so they should be good at that sport!

I'm not surprised Orlando Zender and Hartog Jumpa won the Blindfold Leapfrogging event — they are Junior members of the Leaping Llamas gymnastics team from Mollebamba in Peru. The team holds the record for High-altitude Blindfold Leapfrogging, last year covering 26.3 kilometres in the Andes mountains.

Orlando and Hartog's time was really impressive, but wasn't a world beater. All speed and endurance world records for Low-altitude Blindfold Leapfrogging are held by identical twins Thunder and Lightning Golightly.

In 2008, they chose to leapfrog blindfold across the flat and treeless Black Rock Desert in Nevada, USA, to avoid crashing into any obstacles. They mysteriously vanished after successfully completing a new world record of 37.77 kilometres. Their tracks ended abruptly in the middle of the empty desert without explanation. One theory is that the pair jumped through a hole in the Fabric of Time, and is now blindfold-leapfrogging through the Jurassic era, trying to avoid being eaten by dinosaurs!

I hope the final day goes well, Danny, and you flop to gold!

Best wishes
Eric Bibby
Keeper of the Records

PS I woke up early today, my voice is coming back, my ears aren't droopy, and my purple blotches are fading, which means that by tomorrow the Tasmanian Topsy-Turvy Blotchyosity will be better. We will get to meet at last!

The boys were at the Splatterdrome for the final event of the Silly Olympics: the Wibbly Wobbly Jelly Belly Flop.

'Jimmy Sedgley won a silver medal in the Blancmange Butterfly, and Gracie Green got bronze in the Yogurt Flipper-dash,' said Matthew, showing Danny the updated medal table on his clipboard. 'But we're the only country that's not won a single gold. If  *you* don't do it, we'll come last!'

Danny removed the Silly Sausage from behind his ear and handed it to his friend.

'I won't let Great Britain down,' he said, and strode away to do his final practice flop before the competition began. He was doing 'The Flying Squirrel' – a swooping, twisting dive with arms outstretched.

Danny stood on the edge of the springboard and

stuck out his tummy to get
maximum jelly-to-belly
contact. He bounced
hard on the board,
but sprang too high,
and hurtled towards
the quivering mass
of strawberry jelly in
the pool beneath him.

*Uh-oh!* he thought,
spinning sideways and losing control of his flop.

SPLODGE!!!

In a tumble of flailing arms and legs, Danny's
body slapped into the
firm, red, rubbery
mound.

Natalie
had sneaked
into the
spectators'
gallery to watch
her brother. As he

slipped and slopped to the edge of the flop pool, Danny could hear his sister's laughter echoing through the Splatterdrome.

He hobbled over to Matthew, his face burning as red as the jelly.

'I twisted my knee on jelly-entry,' he winced. 'I'll never be able to climb back up those steps. I'll have to pull out of the event.'

'But you're our last hope for a gold medal,' groaned Matthew. 'Your belly's the floppiest!'

Natalie skipped down the steps towards them. 'That was rubbish!' she sneered.

'Not as rubbish as *you'd* be,' replied Danny, his pride hurting even more than his knee.

'I could belly flop *a million times* better than *that*!'

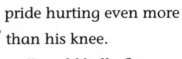

'Prove it! Take my place in the team!' Danny folded his arms and smiled.

'Or are you a cowardy custard?'

'Can't flop for mustard,' added Matthew.

Natalie glared at them, but Danny knew she couldn't back out now. His sister was silent for a few seconds while she thought about it.

'OK, I'll do it,' she snarled. 'But if you tell my friends, your belly really *will* be jelly!'

'I promise,' said Danny, pulling an imaginary zip across his lips.

The boys watched the competition from the stands. There were some great floppers. A boy from Japan did a brilliant 'Plopping Frog' – a high hop from the board with arms and legs stretched wide.

Then came Natalie's turn. Danny couldn't believe it when he heard the announcement. She was going to attempt 'The Hippo' – a twisting double somersault with legs akimbo – probably the hardest jelly belly flop in the world.

Danny held his breath as his sister prepared her flop. She checked her nails, flicked her ponytail, then raced to the end of the diving board and took off . . .

It was a
wonderful
flop. With a
superb, sloppy
SPLAP-P-P-P,

Natalie's belly splattered
the jelly far and wide. The crowd went wild and,
before he knew what he was doing, Danny was on
his feet applauding and whistling for his sister.

He looked towards the judges table. One by one
they held up their scores:

10 . . .

10 . . .

10 . . .

10 . . .

10.

A perfect score! The crowd went *mega*-wild.

As Natalie climbed from the flop pool, she stuck
her tongue out at Danny. 'Told
you I could flop better than you,'
she said, flouncing towards the
changing room.

The final event of the Silly Olympics was over. After lunch everyone crowded in to Penley Park to watch the last chocolate medals being awarded and to see Danny officially close the games.

There was a huge cheer as Natalie stepped on to the winner's podium and 'Beaky' Rogers placed a gold medal around her neck. As the Pots and Pans Orchestra clanged 'God Save the Queen', Danny was sure he could see a tear glistening in his sister's eye.

'Hooray for Nat the Splat!' shouted Matthew.

Danny pulled the Silly Sausage from behind his ear, held it high above his head and shouted, 'I now declare . . .'

He was interrupted by a terrifying voice booming across the park.

'Not on your nelly!'

Mrs Meaney, the Head of the Safety Police, sliced through the crowd like a mighty orange battleship, leaving a bow wave of startled spectators in her wake. Three tree fellers scurried along behind her carrying enormous chainsaws. She scowled at the medal table and the winners' podium set up beneath the tree.

'What's going on?' she yelled.

'The Silly Olympics . . .' began Danny.

Mrs Meaney gasped. 'You mean running and throwing and jumping? That means broken bones!' she yelled, snatching the sausage from

Danny's hand and throwing it on to the grass. 'Silly Olympics! Banned!'

'You're too late!' said Danny. 'The games are over – and not a single bone broken!'

'*What?!* Why didn't Mandy tell me this was going on?' fumed the safety chief, clenching her teeth and growling like a tiger with toothache. She glared at the Duelling Tree as if it was the most horrible thing she had ever seen. 'Chop that down!'

The park was filled with a snarling, howling wail as the men fired up their chainsaws.

'But, Mrs Meaney,' shouted Danny, 'cutting down trees is dangerous. You could break . . . everything!'

The safety police chief gulped. 'You're right!' she said, gesturing to stop the tree fellers. 'I-I . . .' she stuttered. 'Y-you . . .' she stammered.

Her shoulders slumped.

Her head drooped.

Her lip quivered.

'Cutting down trees,' she mumbled miserably. 'Banned!'

A huge cheer exploded from the children.

'Cheering,' muttered Mrs Meaney as she trudged away unhappily. 'You could break your throats . . . banned.'

But the cheering went on.

Mrs Meaney stepped on the Silly Sausage lying on the grass. She slipped, cartwheeled into the air, and crashed down on top of it, her big orange bottom squashing it flat.

'She fell on her nelly!' laughed Matthew.

'Sausage Squishing!' said Danny. 'That's one event we didn't think of!'

# Danny Baker Record Breaker

That evening, as the boys ate their 'Farewell' pie and peas supper, Matthew looked at the final medal table:

## Silly Olympics

### FINAL MEDAL TABLE

|  | gold | Silver | bronze |
|---|---|---|---|
| ALBANIA | 1 | 1 | 1 |
| BELARUS | 1 | 1 | 1 |
| CANADA | 1 | 1 | 1 |
| GREAT BRITAIN | 1 | 1 | 1 |
| GREENLAND | 1 | 1 | 1 |
| INDIA | 1 | 1 | 1 |
| JAPAN | 1 | 1 | 1 |
| MADAGASCAR | 1 | 1 | 1 |
| MEXICO | 1 | 1 | 1 |
| NEW ZEALAND | 1 | 1 | 1 |
| PAPUA NEW GUINEA | 1 | 1 | 1 |
| PERU | 1 | 1 | 1 |

'Awesome!' he said. 'Every country has won exactly the same number of gold, silver and bronze medals!'

'What are the chances of that?' asked Danny.

'About a giga-squig-squillion and ninety-three to one!' laughed Matthew. 'I know, why don't I get the teachers to work it out when they finally realize they can't do my Mega Maths Conundrum?'

Just then, Mum and Dad arrived at the Kids' Camp.

'Bad news, Danny,' said Mum. 'Mr Bibby had to leave this afternoon to attend an emergency meeting about *The Great Big Book of World Records*. He's really sorry you didn't get to meet, but asked you to send him the final day's results.'

Danny went to his tent and scribbled a letter to the Keeper of the Records.

To the Keeper of the Records
The Great Big Book of World Records
London


Dear Mr Bibby


Our Silly Olympics are over, our conker tree is
saved, and I know how to work out the average
distance blancmange will splatter when a 23 kg
girl swims the butterfly in it (4.77 metres).


Manjola Nooja from Albania won that event.
She's had lots of practice – every year her
village celebrates the first day of spring by
swimming in blancmange – Ace!


This morning, Natalie won gold in the Wibbly
Wobbly Jelly Belly Flop.
She was so good at it she
scored a perfect ten
from all five judges! This
MUST be a record!

nat's amazing
belly

I had to pull out of the event at the last minute, so no records for me. Maybe next time!

All the kids taking part in the Making Maths Magic! event said that the Silly Olympics was the most numeracy fun they'd ever had! The organizers have voted to hold the games every four years from now on, with a different country hosting it every time. They're going to pay me and Matt in chocolate coins to show them how to run it! We've already thought of new events to make it even bigger and better next time:

chocolate coins

Cushion Plumping
Paper Scrumpling
Biscuit Dunking
Pea-pod Popping
Can Kicking
Swap-card Flicking and
Mozzarella Conkers

mozzarella conker

It's a pity you had to dash back to London. I really wanted to say hello face to face. But as my grandma says, 'Every cowpat makes a happy worm.' In other

Cowpat and Worm

words, you leaving means I won't have to spend another night in Natalie's pink bedroom. Ace!

Best wishes
Danny Baker
Director of Events, Silly Olympics

PS I've enclosed the final day's results. I hope one of them is a record breaker. I'll be really disappointed if the Silly Olympics hasn't produced any new world records.

ARE YOU A RECORD
BREAKER ?

The Great Big Book
of World Records
London

Dear Danny

I'm glad the Silly Olympics were a success. I
wish I could have been there to experience the
fun!

I'm very sorry I had to rush away without
saying hello or goodbye! The brand-new edition
of *The Great Big Book of World Records* comes
out next week and I had to make sure it was
absolutely up to date with the very latest
records.

At least you didn't have to suffer Natalie's
bedroom again. I know how serious overexposure
to a sister's room can be. Beginning in the
summer of 1998, William Pennybaker of Australia
was forced to share his sister Tammy's bedroom

when his grandma came for a long stay. A record-breaking 589 days and nights of looking at pink walls and furniture, smelling 'pink' perfume and listening non-stop to Tammy's favourite Pink songs finally drove poor Billy mad.

He now spends his days in the Australian outback, living as a hermit in a completely black cave, headbanging to the music of rock band Black Death Warlock and only washing his body with Old Socks shower gel.

I'm delighted to tell you that the last day of the games produced not one, but *four* world records, including one for the Silly Olympics itself!

I managed to get back to my office just in time to make sure that all these records will appear in the new edition of *The Great Big Book of World Records*. I will send you a signed copy to add to your collection.

Well done to you all!

Best wishes

Eric Bibby

Keeper of the Records

THE GREAT BIG BOOK OF WORLD RECORDS

*This is to certify that*

Natalie Baker

holds the world record for:

The Wibbliest Wobbliest Sloppiest Ploppiest

Jelly Belly Flop Ever

(A Perfect 10)

Keeper of the Records

Eric Bibby

World Record Breaker

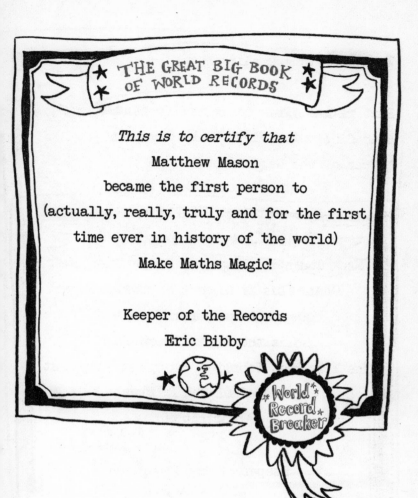

THE GREAT BIG BOOK
OF WORLD RECORDS

*This is to certify that*
Matthew Mason
became the first person to
(actually, really, truly and for the first
time ever in history of the world)
Make Maths Magic!


Keeper of the Records
Eric Bibby

World
Record
Breaker

**THE GREAT BIG BOOK OF WORLD RECORDS**

*This is to certify that*
the First Silly Olympics
produced
the Deadest Dead Heat,
Stalest Stalemate,
Levelest Level-pegging,
Neck-and-neck Ding-dong Competition Ever
(Chance of Occurrence: approximately
one giga-squig-squillion and
ninety-three to one)

Keeper of the Records
Eric Bibby

348

THE GREAT BIG BOOK OF WORLD RECORDS

*This is to certify that*
Daniel 'Danny' Baker
Invented and organized
the World's Most
Twirly, Hurly, Crawly, Dashy, Sloppy,
Splattery, Floaty, Buttery, Kicky, Tricky,
Leapy, Floppy, Wibbly, Wobbly
Silly Olympics
Ever

Keeper of the Records
Eric Bibby

World Record Breaker

When Matthew came round after breakfast, Mum and Dad held a little award ceremony to present Danny, Matthew and Natalie with their certificates.

Natalie fixed the boys with her fiercest stare. 'Remember,' she warned. 'One word to my friends and you're squished.'

'Then you're going to have to squish the *Penleydale Clarion*!' said Dad, holding up that morning's copy of the local newspaper.

# THE PENLEYDALE CLARION

## LOCAL GIRL IS A PERFECT FLOP!

Penleydale's Natalie Baker is a worldwide flopping sensation. She became the first person ever to score a perfect ten, grabbing gold in the Wibbly Wobbly Jelly Belly Flop Silly Olympics final.

Her performance  caught the attention of Percy Painter, manager of the Great  British Jelly Belly Flop team. 'It's a long time since this country produced such a naturally talented flopper,' said Mr Painter last night. 'I want her in my squad for the World Flopping Championships in Tokyo next year.'

'I'm so proud!' said Mum.

'*I'm so doomed!*' moaned Natalie.

'But, Nat,' laughed Danny, 'you should be on top of the world – you're the Flop of the World! Ace!'

# THE WORLD'S
## LOUDEST ARMPIT FART

## STEVE HARTLEY

TO THE MANAGER
The Great Big Book
of World Records
London

Dear Sir,
Yesterday I attempted
the Continuous Musical Armpit-
farting record. I managed to play
2,081 verses of 'Old MacDonald Had a
Farm' before I squeezed too hard
and bruised my fingers.
My sister was upstairs, trying to listen
to her favourite boy band. Even with
the volume turned right up she could
still hear my armpit farts! Could they
have been the Loudest Ever?
        Yours faithfully,
        Danny Baker
(Aged nine and three quarters)

WARNING!
COVER
YOUR
EARS!

Join Danny as he attempts to smash a
load of crazy records, including:

**MESSIEST JELLY FIGHT!**
**CRINKLIEST WRINKLES!**
**VILEST VERRUCAS!**

## OUT NOW!

# THE WORLD'S
## STICKIEST EARWAX

## STEVE HARTLEY

Join Danny as he attempts to smash a
load of wacky records, including:

## DEADLIEST ROLLERCOASTER RIDE!
## FILTHIEST FURBALLS!
## MOST BONKERS BIRTHDAY!

# OUT NOW!

# THE WORLD'S ITCHIEST PANTS

## STEVE HARTLEY

TO THE MANAGER
The Great Big Book
of World Records
London

Dear Sir,
I am going to attempt the
Ant-filled-underwear Endurance
world record. I've stuffed my pants
with ant bait including:
+ three egg and ketchup sandwiches
+ a squishy banana
+ a greasy lamb chop
+ a blob of rhubarb crumble (with
custard)
+ a couple of cockles
Now I'm off to sit in an ant's nest. Ace!
        Yours faithfully,
        Danny Baker
        (Aged ten and a bit)

WARNING!
GROSSEST
RECORDS
YET!

Join Danny as he attempts to smash a
load of madcap records, including:

**LONGEST NOSE-ICICLE!**
**FASTEST FLEA ATTACK!**
**STINKIEST FLU!**

## OUT NOW!

# THE WORLD'S
## WINDIEST BABY

## STEVE HARTLEY

TO THE MANAGER
The Great Big Book
of World Records
London

Dear Sir,
Great news! I think my
brother Joey's going to be a
record breaker just like me!
His trouser-tearing trumps, belly-
busting belches and rip-roaring
raspberries are Mega-Ace! He
won the Fart-propelled Pushchair
competition at playgroup and his burps
can knock cats out of trees!
I'm so proud – is he the World's
Windiest Baby?

Yours faithfully,
Danny Baker
(Aged ten and a half)

WARNING!
MORE
DANNY BAKER
BOOKS
AVAILABLE!

Join Danny as he attempts to smash a
load of hilarious records, including:

## TALLEST PIZZA TOWER!
## BIGGEST UNDERPANT-HAT!
## MOST INFECTIOUS YAWN!

# OUT NOW!

# THE WORLD'S WACKIEST WEBSITE

## DANNY BAKER RECORD BREAKER

Join Danny and author Steve Hartley as they attempt to create the wackiest website ever.

Dear Mr Bibby

I've got a new website! Ace! Now I can tell people what I'm up to, and other kids can tell me about their record attempts. If they're really mega I'll send them certificates and stickers. There's loads of great stuff on the site, like:

- Gross recipes
- The world's stinkiest records
- Awesome activities
- Videos of people breaking records
- Competitions, and loads more!

Could this be the Wackiest Website Ever?

Best wishes

Danny Baker